GOOD
SAM

GOOD SAM

A KATE BRADLEY MYSTERY

DETE MESERVE

Published by Lake Union Publishing, Seattle

www.apub.com

Amazon, the Amazon logo, and Lake Union Publishing are trademarks of Amazon.com, Inc., or its affiliates.

ISBN-13: 9781477809013
ISBN-10: 1477809015

Cover design by Laura Klynstra

Printed in the United States of America

To Paul, Ben, Jake, and Lauren—
the loves of my life

CHAPTER ONE

I don't cover soft news. Stories about lottery winners, runaway brides, weight-loss secrets, or how to beat speeding tickets are given to reporters with a talent for covering these gentler topics. A kind of talent I don't have. Give me a high-speed car chase down the 405 freeway during rush hour, an out-of-control brush fire threatening multimillion-dollar homes in the Hollywood Hills, or a bank robbery shoot-out with police, and I'll turn in a story that'll keep viewers glued to the TV news instead of their smartphones and YouTube.

So after forty-eight hours of covering a commuter train collision that had killed twelve and injured at least another six, I couldn't believe the story I was being assigned. "A Los Angeles resident called to tell us she found a big stack of cash on her front porch this morning," the Channel Eleven news editor, David Dyal, said in the morning assignment meeting. "She thinks it came from a Good Samaritan and is giving us an exclusive on the story."

I assumed he would gesture toward Laurie Evans, the fresh-out-of-journalism-school reporter with a pixie haircut and perfect white teeth who recently had filed a highly emotional report on dogs wearing Halloween costumes. But his finger was pointing at me. "Yours, Kate."

Or at least that's what I thought he'd said. But he couldn't have. Not with the death toll mounting on the train wreck. He was staring right at me, so maybe he was expecting an update. "Actually," I told him, "I'm working on an angle that the train engineer may have been texting minutes before the Metrolink crash."

The room went silent, and all eyes were upon me. Every reporter was thinking the same thing. *Don't question David's assignments, because you'll pay for it—forever.* You may get what you want in the short term, but in the long run, you'll find yourself covering the new dog poop ordinance in Pacoima or the city landfill briefings.

"One of Mel Gibson's sons was injured in the train wreck, so Susan will take over the Metrolink story," David said, running his hands through his unruly black hair.

I glanced over at Susan Andrews, the former Miss Texas reporter who covered celebrity stories and scandals. I couldn't tell whether she was gloating over her assignment or if an overzealous doctor had pumped too much filler into her lips.

Assignment meetings are held in the Fish Bowl, a glass-enclosed conference room in the back of the newsroom, and they are always chaotic and loud, with several discussions going on at once. Most reporters multitask at the meeting, tapping out their required news tweets, catching up with news online, and sometimes even talking on their cell phones. Today was no exception.

"This Good Samaritan story sounds more up your alley, Ted," I called across the room, trying to be heard over the din and motioning to the reporter in the corner who was texting on his BlackBerry.

"I'm covering Palmdale's new ordinance requiring homeowners to keep an attractive front yard," Ted answered.

Ouch. I wondered what Ted had done to warrant such cruel and unusual punishment, but then I remembered that his report on baby smuggling last week was so poorly written that he must have thought grammar was an award given to pop music artists.

On the whiteboard on the front wall of the conference room, David tracked all the stories for the day under four columns: "Follow," "Top

Story," "Breaking News," and "Other." Most of the time, you'd find my name and assignment under "Breaking News." But today, under "Other," he scribbled my name and "Good Sam."

"Kate, all yours," he said, with that silly grin he always had when he was handing out crummy assignments. "Think of this as a twenty-four-hour break from your usual death, destruction, and weeping-survivors' stories."

I didn't want a break from the Bummer Beat. I'm one of the best at covering tragedy, and I'm able to get interviews and shots that others can't. I get them first and I get them on deadline. I had no business covering a soft story like this one.

"Make it interesting, Kate, and we'll run it as the kicker before sports," David said, rolling up the sleeves of his white oxford shirt.

"I can already hear the sound of millions of viewers switching channels," I said, grumbling.

"You'll be thanking me later for this assignment. Trust me."

I'm not good at trust. Trust can break your heart, and if you happen to be one of the victims of the stories I usually cover, trust can kill you.

As I headed to the news van, I had no idea that my life was about to change forever. Sometimes the most important moments in your life can only be seen in the rearview mirror.

A news director once told me I wasn't TV news reporter material. Sure, I had the pedigree, he'd said. The journalism degree from Columbia University and a regional Emmy Award for covering a double murder in La Jolla. The problem, he had declared, was that I didn't *look* like a reporter. I didn't have the "package."

For one thing, I'm not blonde like so many of today's anchors and reporters. And while I wear a fair amount of makeup on-air, I don't heap on the spray tan or the bronzer and lip liner or coat my eyes with fake eyelashes and so much shadow that I should be wearing a sash and tiara instead of holding a microphone. Which brings me to another important difference. Unlike some news reporters, I was never a beauty pageant contestant, and I don't have a title like "former Miss Florida" or "former America's Junior Miss." Nor am I what they call a "news babe," wearing thigh-high skirts and body-hugging blouses, enticing male viewers to watch, even if they're not paying attention to a word I'm saying.

Instead my hair is light brown and cut in a layered, shoulder-length style that's supposed to say "reliable" and "trustworthy," but also "feminine." Thanks to braces in high school, I do have the requisite gleaming white, perfectly aligned teeth, and my eyes are hazel with a hint of copper, which makes them appear uncannily exotic on camera.

Even so, I have something more valuable than the "package." David Dyal calls it "fearlessness." But I'm not fearless. Just persistent. Six years on the Bummer Beat has honed my tenacity. I have scaled smoky hilltops to get the best shot of a wildfire in Griffith Park, crossed crimescene tape to cover a shooting at city hall, and even (stupidly, I admit) chased a suspect down an alley. To be fair, he was unarmed and part of a group of teenagers suspected of burglarizing a celebrity's home for jewelry.

Because I primarily report on the Bummer Beat, I spend a lot of time covering stories in the zone the Los Angeles Police Department calls "South Bureau." The zone covers non-tourist-friendly areas like Watts and the Port of Los Angeles, and its 640,000 residents and 18,000 gang members account for almost 40 percent of LA's homicides each year. Most of these murders don't make it onto TV newscasts unless a child or innocent bystander is involved, but enough stories make it to air that I, along with my cameraman, Josh, know the territory well.

We are well versed in which streets to avoid, which areas might leave the news van vulnerable to tagging if we stopped too long at a traffic light, and most important, which people to avoid. From Cypress

Park to Long Beach, the last thing we want to hear is "Wassup?" from a group of guys wearing baggy pants.

I wasn't surprised that Cristina Gomez, the woman who claimed to have found money on her front porch, lived in South Bureau. I figured the cash had been tossed there as part of a drug deal gone sour.

As we drove to Cristina's house—past run-down strip malls, several recycling yards, and vacant lots littered with trash that had accumulated against their chain-link fences, Josh asked, "How exactly did we end up assigned to this story instead of following up on the train collision? Are we in the doghouse or something?"

I smiled. When I first met Josh, I suspected the Abercrombie & Fitch–clad twenty-seven-year-old with the mop of blond hair was more frat boy than news cameraman. But looks can be deceiving. Turned out he'd been a news junkie since he was a kid. Every day after school, he would listen to the police scanner, and if something interesting happened, he'd grab his 110-film camera and pedal his bike to the scene. Some of his photos even ended up in the *LA Times* before he graduated from high school.

"Maybe David assigned us this story because no one else on the team knows South Bureau like we do," I said.

"No one else will *drive into* South Bureau."

My cell phone rang, and the name "Hale Bradley" flashed on the screen.

"Dad," I answered.

He wasted no time getting down to business. "Katie," he said, "I'm flying to LA on Friday. Can we get together for dinner?"

"Sure. What time and where?"

"I'll have Lisa in my office e-mail you the details."

"What's bringing you—"

"We'll catch up when I see you," he said, cutting me off. "Gotta run now. Much love." He hung up. My dad never said "good-bye" or "take care" or any of the niceties other people used before hanging up.

He thought those words were a waste of time, throwaways that didn't convey actual feeling.

"I still don't get it," Josh said, shaking his head. "Your dad is Hale Bradley, majority leader of the US Senate. One of the most powerful decision makers in the country. Why aren't you covering the political beat for one of the networks instead of chasing breaking news in LA?"

"Breaking news is more honest," I said. "At least when people lie or cheat or steal, they do it out in the open, where we can cover it. In the political world they do much the same thing, except behind closed doors. Besides, a breaking-news story gets double or triple the ratings of any story about politics."

"Does your dad know you think this way?"

"He's always trying to get me into doing political coverage. He wants me to perpetuate what he calls the Bradley family dynasty."

Josh shot me an incredulous look. "Dynasty?"

"My uncle is the mayor of Princeton, New Jersey, and I have a cousin who's running for senator in Maryland."

"So instead of state dinners and fund-raising galas with the Bradleys, you get to be . . . here," he said, and pointed out the window.

Cristina's gray-stuccoed house was fortified behind a chain-link fence. White lace curtains fluttered behind windows covered by thick steel bars. I stood on the sidewalk for a moment and tugged on the sleeves of my jacket, not entirely sure how to cover a soft story like this. A murder, a robbery, a burglary, an accident—those are easy. Collect facts, talk with police, and snare an interview with a victim—if they're not dead. But there had been no crime committed here, and as far as I could tell, there would not be much of a story, either.

In breaking-news situations, the cameraman always stays within a few feet of me, capturing the scene, the events, and the interviews as they unfold in real time. But for stories like this, it's better for the photographer to wait in the van because when a reporter and cameraman show up unannounced, many people will suffer from what we call fight-or-flee syndrome, which makes them slam and lock their doors, refuse interviews, and sometimes call the police. So while Josh readied his camera in the van, I headed to the front door.

I shouldn't have worried about this being a fight-or-flee because before I could even knock, Cristina flung open the door and greeted me with open arms.

"You are Kate Bradley, yes?" she exclaimed, ushering me in.

She was a tiny woman, five feet tall at most, with ink-black hair parted down the middle and sensible eyeglasses. Her home was neat and organized, as though dust and dirt had declared her place off-limits. But the cleanliness couldn't hide the sheer poverty beneath—rips in the sagging furniture, the threadbare rugs, and paint peeling from the ceiling. The place smelled of cooked onions and bleach.

"I found the money yesterday morning," she said with a soft Guatemalan accent. "There was no note. Nothing to tell me who it came from."

I studied her profile. Was she too eager to tell her story? I'd interviewed several people who'd trumped up stories to get attention. One Brentwood woman had faked an entire abduction—putting duct tape over her mouth and hands and lying in the gutter on a street in Compton. Later she admitted to staging the whole thing because she wanted the publicity to kick-start her faltering acting career.

Cristina took me into the kitchen and pointed to twenty stacks of crisp bills arranged neatly on the chipped Formica counter.

She lowered her voice to a reverent whisper. "One hundred thousand."

A hundred thousand dollars. I had expected several hundred dollars—or at best a few thousand. I ran my fingers along the edges of the stacks, letting the magnitude of the number sink in. My voice caught in my throat. "Surely this came from someone you know."

"I asked everyone I could think of, but they say no—they do not know anything about it. Then I thought maybe it came from the Los

Angeles Foundation. My husband, Carlos, is out of work, and we've been getting help from them."

"Could it have come from the foundation?"

She laughed, a girlish giggle that showed off two silver teeth. "The Los Angeles Foundation doesn't give away one hundred thousand dollars to one family."

"Then who do you think is responsible?"

"It's a miracle," she said. "*El espíritu de Dios.* What you call the spirit of God."

She started to cry; big tears formed at the corners of her eyes like glassy jewels.

"This has been a hard time for us. Last month we were robbed. They took so much of what we had—even some of the children's things. And then Carlos was let go from his job working as a janitor at the high school. But to know that someone is looking over us and helping us—it is a miracle."

I handed her a tissue from my purse. With the Oprahization of our culture, perfect strangers often wept when I interviewed them. Over the years I had become prepared for it, carrying tissues and a bottle of antacid tablets.

"That's why I called Channel Eleven," Cristina continued. "I want everyone to know about this miracle."

I glanced out the kitchen window. Two-foot-tall weeds and wild grasses grew in the place of a back lawn. A faded-red Pontiac rusted in the far corner. I don't believe in miracles, but if anyone deserved one, it was this family.

"We are bringing the money to a bank this morning." She reached into a cabinet by the stove and pulled out a large canvas bag. "This is what it came in."

The bag was plain with no distinctive markings, except for a faint number eight stamped on the side.

It looked to me like the Gomez family had received a much-needed gift from a very generous, yet anonymous, friend. Josh and I taped an interview with Cristina, but I seriously doubted it would make it to air at all because of a car chase in West Los Angeles that was chewing up all the airtime.

As we were about to leave, Cristina took my hands in hers, and in a voice barely above a whisper, she said, "You do not believe."

"Believe?"

"I see it in your eyes. You do not believe this is a miracle. But you cannot see everything with your eyes, miss. You have to look in here." She pressed a palm to her heart and closed her eyes.

"I'm not here to judge . . ."

"I'm not the only one to have this miracle happen to them." Her eyes remained closed. "She would not want me to tell you this. Her name is Marie Ellis. She found money, too."

Okay, I was intrigued—not the same level of intrigue I felt covering a murder scene at a celebrity's home or a fire raging through the Palisades, but at least this story now had the makings of what we call a "muffin choker," a bizarre or unbelievable news piece.

"Are you sure you got the address right?" I asked Josh as we turned onto a palm tree–lined street with luxury homes situated on rich green lawns. Many of the homes were true architectural masterpieces with grand entries and lush, perfect landscapes, and every one of them was a gem. Exclusive and expensive.

Josh glanced at his scribbled note. "This is the address Cristina gave us: 625 North Roxbury. Beverly Hills. Even the air smells like money."

I smiled. Many reporters find their cameramen annoying. When you spend concentrated amounts of time with the same person in deadline situations, their habits definitely can get on your nerves. One cameraman I work with, Darren, is always eating beef-and-bean burritos, which make the news van smell like a boys' locker room. Another, Andy, loves to play wall-to-wall indie rock music on Spotify in the van. I like that music, too, but not at brain-numbing decibels. Fortunately for me, Josh didn't have any quirky habits; he was funny, and we struck an easy friendship from the first day we worked together. He was like the cool, slightly younger brother I wished I had, without the bickering that usually goes with that.

We pulled up in front of a rambling Spanish-style house with an orange-tiled roof on a sloping corner lot. In Beverly Hills houses like these sell for upward of four million dollars. How would Cristina Gomez know someone who lived in this kind of estate? As I pressed the polished brass doorbell, I figured Marie Ellis was either the housekeeper or the nanny.

A little girl dressed in a Snow White dress and clutching a Snow White Barbie doll opened the door.

"Someone is here!" she called out.

"Hi, Princess," I said. "I'm Kate Bradley from Channel Eleven. Is Marie Ellis here?"

"She's changing Jasper's diaper." She held out her doll for me to see. "See what I got for my birthday?"

I admired the doll. "Her dress is beautiful. Would you tell Marie I'm here?"

"Marie is my mommy's name," she said, twirling the doll around. "And my middle name, too."

A model-thin woman with a messy ponytail and a baby clutched in her arms rushed into the foyer. Her face fell as she glanced at Josh with his camera and then at me. Clearly we'd made a mistake bringing the camera before I'd had a chance to soften her up for an interview.

"Are you Marie Ellis?" I asked.

She nodded, turning pale.

"Kate Bradley. From Channel Eleven. We received a report that you found a hundred thousand dollars on your front porch."

She sighed. "You've talked to Cristina."

"She thinks it's a miracle."

"Well, I don't want anyone to know about it. In fact I insist that you not mention me or my family in your report."

Her sharp tone startled the baby, and he started to wail. In a flash that seemed to defy the laws of physics, she pulled a pacifier out of her shirt pocket and popped it into the baby's mouth. Instant silence.

"Would you talk with me off the record then?" I motioned to Josh to put down the camera.

She hesitated for a moment and then lowered her voice a notch. "We don't think it's any miracle. We think someone made a serious mistake and we expect they'll return any moment to reclaim their money."

"You don't think a Good Samaritan is involved?"

She shook her head. "Michael, my husband, is the head of neurology at St. Joseph Hospital. Look around. We don't exactly need help from a Good Samaritan."

I glanced at the midnight-blue Mercedes convertible in her driveway. Unless this Good Samaritan was as nearsighted as Mr. Magoo, he couldn't possibly have mistaken this family as needy.

"How do you know Cristina Gomez?"

"She was my housekeeper a few years ago. This morning she called and asked if I had given her a hundred thousand dollars, and I told her I'd found the same amount on my front porch. Now I wish I hadn't."

"Was the money in a canvas bag with the number eight on it?"

"It was in a bag, but I don't remember if there was any number on it," she said.

"Would you mind checking?"

The pacifier fell out of the baby's mouth, and he wailed again. Marie picked it up and tried to slip it back into his mouth, but this time he wouldn't take it. The crying grew louder, and then the little girl came to the door crying, too.

"Mommy, I lost my doll shoes."

"I have to go," Marie said, and without another word, she closed the door.

If she had been the victim of a crime or a witness to one, I would have pressed harder to get an interview. But it's not a crime to find one hundred thousand dollars on your front porch, no matter how rich you are. Besides, this was a feel-good report, certainly not one that warranted guerrilla-style interview tactics.

Still, none of this made sense. If a Good Samaritan really were involved, why would he give money to both the needy and the wealthy?

"What if this Good Sam isn't doing this for good?" I asked Josh as we headed to the van.

"Someone who's given away two hundred thousand dollars sounds good to me—like someone I'd like to meet."

"Maybe there was a time when people went around doing things to help other people, but I think the days of the Good Samaritan are over. The guy we think is a Good Samaritan is probably scamming us."

Josh placed the camera in its case and snapped it closed before we climbed into the van. "How long have we been working on the Bummer Beat together? Almost a year, right? At every accident or disaster, you're always trying to find the people who are working to make the situation better—the helpers. This Good Samaritan giving money away is one of the helpers, Kate."

I wanted to agree with him, but I knew better. "Lots of people appear to be Good Samaritans when in reality they aren't. Remember the story we covered last month about the teenager who rescued four people from a burning apartment building in Pomona?"

He nodded. "He got a medal from the fire department."

"Everyone hailed him as a hero until they found evidence he had started the fire."

Josh frowned and started the van.

"How about the story we covered about the guy who was helping people fix their cars that had broken down in parking lots around the city?" I continued. "Then we found out that he had disabled the cars when the owners were away and offered to fix their cars for a small 'donation.'"

"Okay, you got me," Josh said. "But even you have to admit that this is different. For the first time, we're covering a story where no one is dead, injured, or in a hostage situation. There's no threat at all. Why can't you see this as someone just doing something good?"

I thought about that for a moment. "Maybe I've lost that ability."

My report about Good Sam aired on the noon cast, a sixty-second story to help viewers forget the previous twenty minutes of murder and mayhem before we started talking about the weather.

CHAPTER TWO

A dozen long-stemmed white roses wrapped in white paper and silk ribbon were waiting for me on my desk when I returned to the station that afternoon. I slipped the card off the plastic stem, crumpled it without reading it, and buried it deep in my trash. Then I walked across the reporters' bullpen in the center of the newsroom and placed the flowers on one of the news interns' desks.

I'd done this every time I'd received flowers from him. One of the interns asked me once if I knew who had left expensive flowers on her desk, but I feigned ignorance. I didn't want to explain why I was giving away flowers from my fiancé.

Ex-fiancé. We had broken up six months ago, but Jack couldn't wrap his head around the idea that we were never getting back together. At first I'd assumed that if I didn't return his phone calls or acknowledge the flowers, he'd stop trying. But Jack was used to getting what he wanted, and my ignoring him didn't discourage him.

The newsroom's receptionist hailed me from across the bullpen. "Kate, there's a man on the phone asking for you. He's rambling on about a Good Samaritan or something."

No wonder we ranked fourth in the market. Our own employees didn't even watch our newscasts. "Thanks, Ann. You can put him through." I waited for her to transfer the call.

"Kate Bradley?" the man on the phone said. His voice was full and deep, almost chocolate in its smoothness. "Saw your report about Good Sam today. Have any idea who's behind it?"

"Not yet," I said. "Can I get your name?"

"Rather not say. Do you *actually* think there's some kind of Good Samaritan behind this?"

"Probably not," I said. "It could be some kind of marketing promotion. Maybe a radio station or an Internet start-up giving away money to get publicity."

"They do that?"

"Last month Gnarly.com staff members stood on a street corner in Manhattan in the middle of rush hour and handed out twenty-dollar bills with an announcement about their new outsourcing service. They gave away ten thousand dollars in an hour and got ten times the value of that in marketing exposure."

"That's fine for ten thousand. But what does anyone hope to gain from giving away three hundred thousand dollars?"

"Actually Good Sam has only given away two hundred thousand," I replied.

"Two hundred doesn't include me. I found a hundred thousand dollars on my front porch this morning, too."

I gripped the phone tightly. "What is your name?"

"He left a note with the money."

I scribbled a giant question mark on my notepad. "What did the note say?"

"It says, 'This is for Lauren to go to law school.' Lauren's my daughter."

I put down my pen. "Does she want to go to law school?"

"She got accepted at Georgetown last fall, but I'm on a pension, and she doesn't earn enough as a second-grade teacher to afford it."

"Do many people know that your daughter wants to go to law school?"

"Just about everyone she knows."

"Can you think of anyone who might've wanted to help her get there?"

"Lots of people want to help. But they don't have a hundred thousand dollars to give away," the man said with a chuckle. "You got any idea who's behind all this?"

"Not yet. But I'd like to record an interview with you."

Silence. Then he cleared his throat. "Can't do that. If people knew we got a windfall like this, there'd be no end to the calls and e-mails asking for a piece of it."

The muscles in my shoulders tensed like they always did when I was on the verge of losing an important interview. "There's not much of a story if I can't talk to you on camera."

He didn't answer.

"Will you reconsider?" I continued.

More silence. He had hung up.

Channel Eleven offers its newsroom employees quite a few perks. We get free tickets to movies distributed by our movie studio parent company, and at Christmas we get discounts on used cars at one of the mega car dealers that buys commercial time during our afternoon talk shows. But the perk everyone covets the most is the Cellini. Time after time this gleaming hunk of chromed steel in the newsroom kitchen brews up a perfect, frothy confection of milk and espresso; topped with whipped cream and sprinkled with just the right touch of cinnamon, it's pure heaven.

I had just started on my third perfect cup and was scrambling to finish a story about Good Sam for the Channel Eleven website when Alex, one of the intern reporters, rushed over to my desk. He was dressed in the standard intern uniform: khaki pants pressed a little too carefully, a button-down shirt, and Converse tennis shoes.

"This just came over the scanner. Police were called to the scene of a robbery-assault in Westwood."

I kept typing. "Anyone injured? Dead?"

"No, but—"

"Is a current or former celebrity involved?"

"No."

"Do we have photos? Cell phone video?"

He shook his mop of shaggy brown hair.

"Not much of a story then." I drained the rest of my espresso and stood.

"The only thing is—"

"Look, Alex," I interrupted, "if we reported every robbery that happened in LA, there wouldn't be any time left for important stuff. Like celebrity news. And if we don't make time for celebrity news, we don't sell commercials. And if we don't sell commercials, we don't have jobs."

I started to walk away. I knew I sounded like a blowhard, but I hoped I had conveyed an important lesson about what kinds of stories were newsworthy at Channel Eleven.

"I heard on the scanner that the victim was assaulted because the thief was trying to steal a large canvas bag from his front porch. I guess the homeowner put up one heck of a fight and the burglar didn't get away with it."

"Where's the story in that?" I said over my shoulder.

"I thought it might be related to your Good Sam story. You know, because of the canvas bag on the front porch."

I whirled around. "Smart thinking. I'm impressed," I said, with my best crow-eating smile. "Where are you going to school, Alex?"

"Northwestern University." He handed me a Post-it note. "I took down the address. You think I could work on this Good Sam story with you?"

Interns don't usually get assigned to individual stories or specific reporters. They work wherever they're needed most each day—usually researching story ideas, retrieving video, answering phones, or working on scripts. But Alex clearly had strong reporter instincts, and he was bold enough to ask me for an assignment, something most interns rarely do.

"Definitely. I'll get David to assign you to me and this story."

As Josh and I raced to the address Alex had given me, my phone flashed with a text from my father. Well, actually it came from his assistant because my dad definitely doesn't send text messages. It read: *NY Times says LA is hit-and-run capital of US.*

If there's any bad news about Los Angeles, my dad always lets me know about it. From his perspective, the city is filled with shallow, celebrity-obsessed people who lounge on the beach and regularly dodge bullets from gang members, get stuck in snarled traffic, and breathe smog-choked air.

But that's not the Los Angeles I live in. Yes, LA is a place of gorgeous beaches and paradise weather, but it's also a reporter's dream with its mudslides, wildfires, and earthquakes. Millions live well below the poverty line, and many thousands are in gangs, yet LA is also home to one of the world's greatest concentrations of millionaires and billionaires. Which makes it a city where anything can—and does—happen. An ordinary news day can include a brush fire, a celebrity meltdown, a big-rig crash, a dead body on a hiking trail, a freeway chase, *and* a dust storm.

"This is it," Josh said, interrupting my thoughts. We pulled in front of a modest one-story home, a brown bungalow with a broad front porch. But what distinguished this bungalow from all the others on this quiet street in West Los Angeles was its lawn. The grass was the deep emerald green that you would see on the East Coast, where they get rain year-round. Seriously, it looked like something out of *Better Homes and*

Gardens—there wasn't a single weed or blade of crabgrass growing anywhere, and the edges looked as though they'd been trimmed by hand. I'd seen grass this perfect once in front of a condo building in Beverly Hills. But that stuff turned out to be artificial grass. I leaned down to touch it; this was the real deal.

Josh waited in the van again while I headed for the front door. Given that the man we hoped to interview had scuffled with a thief, we both suspected he wouldn't be nearly as welcoming as Cristina Gomez had been, and we didn't want him to slam the door when he saw the camera. When there was no answer at the front door, I walked down the driveway to the backyard. A white-tiled pool glittered in the late afternoon sun. Most people would have thought it a beautiful sight: pale blue water, its surface rippling in the light breeze. But after my near-drowning experience last month, I hated water and all its camouflage. Oceans, lakes, swimming pools—I despised them all. Water had nearly claimed me once, and I was certain that, given the chance, it would attempt to finish what it had started.

"What are you doing back here?" A voice startled me from behind.

I swung around to see a thin man standing on the back porch. He was about my dad's age, with a neatly trimmed beard and silver wire-rimmed glasses.

I walked toward him and extended my hand. "Hi, I'm Kate Bradley from Channel Eleven."

He looked at my hand but didn't shake it.

"I understand police were called here because of a robbery-assault," I continued.

His face darkened. "I already talked to another reporter about it. From Channel Four. Anna Hernandez."

Damn. Anna Hernandez, the guerrilla reporter. Anna could take even the simplest fender bender and sensationalize it into a matter of national security. I had no doubt she'd position this story of a foiled robbery into something akin to a standoff in the *Die Hard* movie franchise.

Once, when doing a story about carjacking, she stood in the middle of Hollywood Boulevard, yanking open the passenger doors on unsuspecting drivers to illustrate how vulnerable we all were to potential carjackers.

"I'm not here about the robbery. I'm here about the contents of the bag on your front porch."

He dismissed me with a wave of his hand. "Just some old clothes. Nothing valuable. I already told Anna and the police all that."

I motioned toward the small red-and-black bruise by his right eye. "Looks like you put up a big fight to keep the guy from stealing your 'old clothes.'"

He rubbed his face. "Probably shouldn't have . . ."

"My guess is that bag contained a hundred thousand dollars in cash, and there was a lopsided number eight stamped on it."

He fixed a pair of steel-gray eyes on me. "How could you possibly know that?"

"I've interviewed three others who also found one hundred thousand dollars on their front porch. It was on the Channel Eleven news yesterday and today. We're calling him Good Sam, short for 'Good Samaritan.'"

"I don't really watch Channel Eleven much. The anchors shout too much."

I frowned. Could that be why we ranked fourth? "Why would someone want to give you so much money?"

"No idea. I thought there'd been some mistake when I found the money. But the bag was addressed to me."

I straightened. "Could I see it?"

He stepped back inside for a moment and brought back an empty canvas bag. On the side was the same lopsided eight I'd seen on Cristina's bag, but pinned to the bag was a note written in careful block letters. It read, "Dr. K."

"Dr. K?"

"Most people mispronounce my last name, so I have them call me 'Dr. K.' Easier than Kryvoskya."

"Then whoever gave you this money must be someone you know."

He combed his fingers through thin waves of gray hair. "That's a lot of people. Factoring in all my students and people I've met in twenty years of teaching, I'd say we're talking about a potential pool of ten thousand."

"You're a teacher then?"

"I'm a professor in the entrepreneur program at UCLA's Anderson School."

"Can you think of anyone who had the means to give you a hundred thousand dollars?"

"Plenty of my former students have the ability to give away that kind of money. But I can't think of a single one who had a reason to give it to me." He glanced at his watch. "Look, you're wasting your time with me. Larry Durham also got money. And he saw the man."

"He saw Good Sam?"

"Says he did."

I scribbled the name in my notebook. "How do you know Larry?"

"He's done carpentry work around my house over the years. He called me this morning, asking if I knew anything about the money he found on his front porch. He actually thought I might have had something to do with it. Me, on a college professor's salary!"

It was well past five when Josh and I reached Larry Durham's home in Hollywood, a faded brown one-story house that sat behind a tired front lawn and a sagging wooden fence that had seen its best days during the Reagan years.

While Josh readied his camera equipment, I started up the sidewalk to the front door. As I reached the front porch, a man rushed out, shrugging on a denim jacket as he pressed a cell phone to his ear. He appeared to be in his midthirties with closely cropped hair and a curved barbell piercing above his left eyebrow. I opened my mouth to say something, and he put up his hand.

"I'll be there in under thirty," he said into the phone. Then he slipped it into his pocket. "If you're here to give me your *Watchtower* literature, you're wasting your time."

I glanced at my black jewel-neck jacket and tailored Donna Karan pants and couldn't see why he thought I was a door-to-door Jehovah's Witness.

"Actually I'm from Channel Eleven." I waited as my words sunk in. Most people brighten when they hear I'm from a TV station, hopeful at the possibility of being on the news.

Larry wasn't most people. "And?"

"We heard you found a hundred thousand dollars here on this porch. Can we talk about it?"

He met my question with stony silence. "Rather not," he said finally, slipping his other arm into his jacket and shaking it on.

"Can I ask why?"

"You can ask. But I gotta run." He brushed past me and loped toward a faded-green Oldsmobile Cutlass.

I followed him to the car. "I only need a few minutes of your time," I implored through the window.

He rolled down the window. The edge of a blue tattoo peeked out over the neckline of his T-shirt. "Look. I don't want to be on TV. I'm out of work. I don't want people knowing my situation."

I flashed him a pleading look, a hint of a flirty smile. "What situation is that?"

He pulled a pack of cigarettes from his jacket pocket. "Hurt my back a while ago. Laid me up for three months. No one wants to hire a carpenter on the injured list."

"So someone put a lot of money on your front porch to help you out. A Good Samaritan perhaps. Any idea who it was?"

He lit his cigarette. "Could've been lots of people."

"You know many people who would help you out with a hundred thousand dollars?"

"That's the thing. I never told anyone I needed money." He gripped the steering wheel. "No one knows I'm out of work."

"Surely someone knew. Someone in your family, a friend—"

"I never told anyone."

I straightened. "Dr. K says you saw the man who put the money on your porch. Is that true?"

"Yeah." He turned the key in the ignition. The car chugged for a few seconds, then it started. "But it was dark—after midnight—and I only caught a glimpse of him. By the time I opened the door, he was gone."

"Would you talk to me on camera?" My breath was caught up high in my throat. I had a feeling his answer would be "no."

"Can't. Gotta run."

"Can I level with you, Larry?" I said, lowering my voice to a half whisper. "If I don't get this interview, my assignment editor is going to consign me to stories about baby zoo animals and lightning-bolt survivors."

He shrugged and put the car in gear. "At least you've got a job."

Okay, so that approach wasn't working. "Look at it this way," I said. "Other stations are already on this story, and it's only a matter of time until they track you down. Do you really want swarms of reporters descending on your house like locusts at all hours of the day and night? Or do you want to do an exclusive interview with me and get it over with?"

He thought about it for a moment, then he turned off the car. "Three minutes. That's it. If you're not done in three, I'm taking off."

Minutes later I had a microphone in my hand and Josh was pointing a camera at Larry. After years on the Bummer Beat, I'd become adept at nabbing quick sound bites from hurried interviewees. There's an adrenaline rush that comes with it, akin to what a day trader must feel when she sees her stock start to take off or what a basketball player experiences when he throws the ball from the three-point line. In that moment, anything is possible.

But I was also worried. With his tattoos, pierced eyebrow, and tough demeanor, Larry Durham wasn't exactly the kind of person you see in TV news interviews, unless he'd been arrested for a crime.

"Larry, you found one hundred thousand dollars on your front porch this morning," I said, opening the interview. "Do you have any idea who might have given it to you?"

He shook his head. "Nope."

"Why do you think you were singled out to receive the money?"

"No idea."

I bit my lip. If he continued with one-word or two-word answers, I'd have to work miracles with the editor to make this interview worthwhile.

"Do you think there could be a Good Samaritan behind it?"

"Nah. Los Angeles isn't the kind of place where you'd find a Good Samaritan. You hear about those kinds of things happening over the holidays in small towns, where people know each other. Not in a big city like this in the dead of January."

I smiled. I couldn't have written a better intro for this story if I'd had all day to think about it. "What are you going to do with the money?"

"Pay off my bills, save a little. Maybe give some of it away."

"Some of the other recipients of Good Sam's generosity found the number eight on the bags with the money. Was there a number eight on your bag too?"

"I didn't see if there was or not."

"Does that number mean anything to you?"

A strange look brushed across his face for a brief instant, but then he shook his head.

"Are you certain?" I pressed.

"Yeah, I'm sure." He glanced at his watch. "Time's up."

The Good Sam story aired four minutes into the all-important six o'clock newscast. I watched on one of the dozen or so monitors scattered throughout the newsroom. One of the anchors, Kelley Adams, introduced the report.

"Under cover of darkness, he drops one hundred thousand dollars in cash on the front porch, leaving no clues to his identity," Kelley announced. "Who is the mysterious Good Samaritan who has given away nearly half a million dollars to local residents? Channel Eleven's Kate Bradley is in Hollywood with the latest."

There I was standing in front of Larry Durham's house with chunks of concrete missing from his front steps and a battered aluminum screen door as a backdrop.

"Throughout the day on this station's newscasts and on other news programs around the country, we report on the frightening, the grim, the tragic," I said, in the taped report. "We tell you about acts of crime, cruelty, violence, and trauma with headlines like 'Neighbors Mourn Deaths of Six Children' or 'Man Drowns in Freak Accident.' But what you're going to see next isn't that kind of story."

"That's my Katie!" someone said from behind. I didn't need to turn around to realize who it was.

"Dad!" I said, hugging him briefly. "I thought we were having dinner *tomorrow*."

"We are. But I was in the area and thought I'd swing by and see if you were here."

My dad never changed. Even at age sixty-two, he still had a thick head of wavy hair, only a little grayer than I remembered. Despite all the dinners and lunches out and the high-powered events he attended, he'd managed to stay surprisingly trim. When I was a kid, he used to take me on five-mile runs, and I had to push to keep up with him. Now, I imagined, he probably had slowed down a little, but clearly he was still staying in shape.

"I'm having dinner with the head of the California Democratic Party and some of his officers tonight." He brushed a speck of lint from his tailored brown merino wool suit. "I was hoping you'd join me."

I frowned. "I already have dinner plans. And you know how much I love spending the evening listening to political talk."

"You might actually find this dinner interesting. Election season is almost here, and a few key California congressional seats are going to be up for grabs."

"So they brought you out here to get your opinion on who should run and who can win."

"That's the drill." He put his arm around my shoulder. "Katie, you know, now would be a perfect time to segue into a political beat at CNN. Dan Rawlings there keeps asking me when you're going to stop covering breaking news out here and come work for him on the political beat."

"I actually like what I'm doing here."

"Reporting on child abductions, bomb threats, gang shootings, murders—Katie, you're much smarter than that."

This wasn't the first time my dad had registered his disapproval of my career choices. In fact, he managed to make it a part of nearly every one of our conversations in recent months. As he entered his sixties, I think it began to weigh more heavily on him that his only child wasn't following in his political footsteps. Last month, he had paved the way for an interview to work the political desk at MSNBC. Now he was working on a job for me at CNN. At this rate, he'd have me hosting a Sunday morning political show before the year was over.

"Dad," I said, trying hard not to let him know he was getting under my skin, "I'd like to think I'm covering the stories where the criminal gets caught, the person in trouble gets rescued, and the house in the midst of the mudslide is saved. I'd like to think that maybe amid all the violence and cruelty, I'll find some good in this world. The first responders on the scene. The people who catch the suspects. The average guy who helps out the stranger . . ."

His expression softened. "You remind me of your mother when you talk like that. She would be so proud of how you turned out." He paused, and then his tone brightened. "I am proud of you, too. And the upcoming election is shaping up to be one of the most newsworthy in a long time and I don't want you to miss this opportunity to cover it. Think about it, and let me know when I can call Dan at CNN."

I squeezed his hand. "Okay, I'll think about it."

He left a few minutes later, after pressing several crisp fifty-dollar bills into my hand and giving me a quick peck on the cheek. It had been a habit of his since I was little. The amount of money changed, but thankfully my dad hadn't changed much at all.

I was on my way out of the newsroom a few minutes later when Judy, the nighttime receptionist, stopped me. "A man named Jack Hansen called for you. He wanted me to tell you . . ." She glanced at the notes she'd taken. "He's back in town from New York and wanted to see if you'd meet him at The Ivy at eight."

"Would you call him back and let him know I can't make it?" I fired back. Then I felt bad for putting her in the middle. Judy had been a receptionist at Channel Eleven for thirty-two years. She'd been working for the news department before there were computers in the newsroom, before we did live reports from remote locations, before women report-ers got much airtime. So she took this business seriously, never gossiped, and never got involved in anyone's personal life.

"He told me you'd say that," she said efficiently. "And when you did, I was supposed to tell you to meet him for cream and toast." She glanced at her notes again. They were written in shorthand, so I couldn't fathom how she could read them. "No, that was cinnamon toast."

I didn't mean to smile, but one crept across my face anyway. The night I'd met Jack nearly three years ago, we had eaten cinnamon toast.

The way Jack tells it, he saw me from across a crowded restaurant and "knew instantly he had to get to know me." Even though I was already on a date with someone else, he came over, introduced himself, and whisked me away to a French bistro, where we talked through the night.

That's not exactly what happened.

I had just started seeing Rich Hendricks, an investment banker specializing in Asian markets. He was good-looking in a Christian Bale kind of way, smart and ambitious, but he couldn't get through dinner without taking at least three calls on his cell phone. I should say he couldn't get through dinner without *shouting* through at least three calls. If he had been shouting in Italian or French, I might have found it a little sexy. But there's very little to find appealing about a white guy shouting in Japanese all the way through a three-course dinner.

That night, as I picked at my grilled salmon and listened to Rich's end of yet another conference call with the Japanese, someone tapped me on the shoulder.

I turned to look into a tanned face framed by a corona of unruly ash-brown curls. "Excuse me, ma'am," he said, laying on a gusher of a Southern drawl. "Aren't you Kate Bradley from Channel Eleven?" He extended a strong hand. "I'm Jack Hansen. I've wanted to meet you ever since Rich brought you to the company picnic in July."

Turned out we had more in common than I'd expected, because as the son of former treasury secretary William Hansen, Jack also knew firsthand the perks and the pitfalls of growing up in a family of politicians and politics. I also was charmed by a man who knew how to hold up his end of the conversation without a cell phone glued to his ear, but I kept wondering why Rich didn't object, why he didn't ask his coworker to leave his date alone.

Rich covered the mouthpiece of his cell phone and whispered, "This call is going to take a while. Why don't you two order dessert?"

"I think Kate is ready to go," Jack said.

Under ordinary circumstances, I would have been irritated if a man spoke for me. But Jack said it with a good ol' boy finesse that made it sound playful and casual.

"Catch up with you later, Kate." Rich rose, his cell phone still pressed to his ear, planted a quick kiss on my cheek, and sent me on my way.

His comfort with the situation perplexed me. At a French bistro around the corner, everything became clear.

"So you and Rich work together?" I asked Jack.

"You could say that," he said. "I'm Rich's boss. Actually, his boss's boss's boss. My father and I started the firm five years ago."

Rich had been so consumed with impressing the owner with how hard he was working that he hadn't realized the guy had horned in on his date. Then again, maybe he didn't care.

Our waitress, a sliver of a woman with fine gray hair spun into a tall bun that defied gravity, stopped by again. "Have you decided what you'd like yet?" The key word was *yet*, as we'd been sitting there for nearly half an hour and hadn't ordered anything.

"Nothing for me," I said.

"Oh, come on." Jack prodded. "Live a little."

"Really, I'm full."

"If you weren't full," he asked, a twinkle in his eye, "what would be your favorite food of all time?"

I hesitated for a moment, but there was no real contest in my mind. "Cinnamon toast."

"Not on the menu," the waitress snapped.

"I'm sure your chef back there knows how to make cinnamon toast," Jack said, all southern gentleman charm. And when Jack turns on the charm, I swear he could buy and sell the diamonds off the back of a rattlesnake. "Would you ask him to make us both a piece, please? We sure do appreciate your kindness."

The receptionist brought me back to the moment. "Would you like me to call Mr. Hansen back and let him know you can't make it?"

"Yes, please tell him I'm unavailable," I said, louder than I had intended. I wasn't going to meet Jack for cinnamon toast tonight. It would stir up too many memories. Things I didn't want to feel.

I met my friend Teri for dinner instead.

"I loved your story about Good Sam," she said over hot French dip sandwiches at a café around the corner from the station. "It made me cry."

"You cry over greeting card commercials."

I'd known Teri ever since we'd yawned through American history class together at Columbia University, and she was the sentimental type even then. If she didn't have her nose in an Emily Brontë novel, she was watching classic weeper movies like *Terms of Endearment* and *A Walk to Remember*. She even looked like a romance-novel leading lady, with glossy, honey-streaked curls and high cheekbones. After college, Teri applied for a creative position at the Hallmark Channel and was offered the job just seven minutes into her interview. She suspected they hadn't made their decision on the basis of her degree in English literature or her minor in French literature, but had simply chosen her because of her resemblance to a heroine from a Jane Austen novel. "Your story proves there's good in the world," she said. "People are out there doing selfless acts of kindness."

I shook my head. "I'm not sure he's selfless. I mean, why does someone give away large sums of money?"

"Because they want to help people."

"Because they want something in return."

Her dark brown eyes lit up. "What would that be?"

"Attention."

"It's not a crime to get attention for helping people, is it?"

I fiddled with my ring. "No, but he'll use the attention to get something else he wants."

She poured herself some more wine, and I motioned to fill my glass, too. "To be honest, I think viewers would prefer to think this is the work of a Good Samaritan, not some kind of marketing gimmick."

"Unfortunately, this is the news I'm doing. Not story time. We don't tell viewers what they'd *like* to hear. We try to uncover the truth."

She paused, tilted her head. "Seems like ever since you and Jack broke up, you're becoming more cynical," she said softly.

I considered this for a moment. There was some truth to it, of course. But it wasn't the breakup that was making me look at things with a skeptic's eye. The world was changing. Mass shootings, bombings, multibillion-dollar Ponzi schemes, sex trafficking, long lists of politicians taking bribes, and investment bankers convicted of massive fraud. The list was endless. Even though I only covered a fraction of these stories, there was no doubt the world felt more troubled—less good—with every new headline.

Teri drove a fork into dessert, a rosy baked apple scented with cinnamon. "He was quoted again in the *Wall Street Journal* yesterday. Did you see the article?"

"Nope," I said. I knew which "he" she was talking about.

"He was named *Investmentline*'s Fund Manager of the Year. His company's doing well, too."

I wanted to change the subject to something other than Jack Hansen. But how? "Sounds like a puff piece."

"Not entirely. They said his tough management style attracts clients and gets results but leaves behind a trail of people who don't trust him."

"No surprise there."

"Is he still calling you?" she asked gently.

"He still calls and leaves messages. Send flowers every few weeks." I slid my fingertips along the rim of my glass, comforted by the smooth, repetitive motion. "He's in town and asked to meet me for dinner tonight."

Teri frowned. "You should have gone. Honestly I don't understand why you two don't just get back together already."

We were silent then, both of us gazing into our drinks. The first time Teri had met Jack, she had instantly fallen under his spell. On the surface I could see why. He was everything many women look for— good-looking but not overly so, intelligent, successful, and charming. He had the brash manner of someone who had been born into privilege and connections and politics, yet he didn't flaunt it.

But if you chipped away at the veneer, Jack was a liar, plain and simple. "Shading the truth" was an essential part of his job in the investment banking business, but it didn't stop there. He lied about the mundane and the inconsequential, too. He'd tell me he was going to the office, but he'd spend the morning on the golf course instead. He'd say he was working late to crunch numbers, but he was really taking clients out to dinner and drinks.

You can overlook lies like that if you want to. Other lies hit you square in the face, knock you off your feet, and suck the life breath out of you. One night after finishing work early, I decided to surprise Jack at his downtown office. I had come bearing chorizo-and-olive paella takeout from Ciudad, but when the elevator doors opened, there was Jack kissing Ashley Holloway, another investment banker in the firm.

"It's not what it looked like," Jack said. Then he went on to say that Ashley had been distraught about a fight with her fiancé, and when he gave her a hug to comfort her, she was the one who had initiated the kiss.

I might have forgiven him if he hadn't concocted such an elaborate lie. It was only a kiss after all. But if he thought I was dumb enough to buy his story then, there was no telling what other whoppers he would tell later on.

"The way I see it," Teri said. "Jack apologized for what he did. And he swore it would never happen again, right?"

I glanced at my lap and realized I had twisted my napkin into a tight knot. "I just don't trust him."

"There isn't any guy out there who's truly good all the time," Teri said with a sigh. "Unless you're looking to marry Gandhi."

"He's dead."

"See what I mean?"

CHAPTER THREE

Three times a week, more often if I'd overindulged at dinner, I ran 3.2 miles around Lake Hollywood early in the morning. The morning after my dinner with Teri, I decided to run the loop twice. There's no faster way to end your career as a news reporter than gaining ten pounds eating late-night pasta dinners and profiteroles.

Lake Hollywood isn't really a lake, it's a man-made dam and reservoir—and it's not technically in Hollywood, either. But it's as close as we get to nature smack in the center of the city. And it's where I do my best thinking.

I've been a runner for as long as I can remember. When my father and I weren't discussing American history, current events, or voting trends, we were running through parks, alongside train tracks, on the beach, and on craggy mountain trails. I ran my first 5-K race when I was in second grade.

Now running has become an almost meditative way to think about the stories I'm working on. But even on the second loop, I couldn't get my mind off Good Sam. As much as I had initially grumbled about the assignment, I found myself returning again and again to think about it. Somewhere out there in this vast city, someone was doing something generous and good. And for a brief moment in the midst of a string of reports on a crime rampage on Hollywood Boulevard, a shutdown of the 5 freeway, a politician resigning in the wake of a sexual harassment scandal, and a bomb threat at the airport, we were able to devote a lot of airtime to it.

But stories like Good Sam don't last in today's news world. Unfortunately, Good Sam was what we call a fly-by-night, a soft news story without staying power. Like cotton candy, fly-by-nights dissolve before viewers can form any reaction.

After I finished my run, I showered and dressed, and then I drove to the station. I walked into the newsroom to find a group of reporters and interns gathered in David's office instead of the Fish Bowl.

"Two hundred and twelve e-mails, one hundred and nine comments on the website," David was saying. "It got hundreds of comments on our Facebook page . . ."

"What's he talking about?" I whispered to Alex.

"The Good Sam story," Alex said.

"Are you kidding me?" I said.

"Some people are offering tips for finding him," David continued, scanning through a list on his computer. "A few are thanking us for reporting on good news for a change. Most are telling tales of woe—lost jobs and family tragedies, huge medical bills, that kind of stuff. Others are writing about their unfulfilled dreams, of needing down payments for new homes, wishing for cosmetic dentistry and even plastic surgery. Nearly all of them ask us to pass their requests on to Good Sam."

Good Sam was not a fly-by-night.

"The story's all over CNN and everywhere on the Internet," David said. "The *Wall Street Journal* ran a piece about Good Sam, saying they admired him but thought he'd be better off giving money through a charitable foundation and getting the tax deduction. Everyone's got a theory about who he is. There's even a video on FunnyorDie.com saying that Good Sam is Snooki from *Jersey Shore*."

I tapped on Twitter on my smartphone. I'd often wondered how effective our station's tweets were at generating viewer interest in a story. Between taking still photographs at the scene to post on the website, writing up stories to post on the website, and posting our tweets, it was often daunting to fit everything in on tight broadcast deadlines. But Channel Eleven required tweets from all its reporters, even if most of the time only one or two of our followers responded to them.

That wasn't the case for #GoodSam. I stared at the screen. Seventy-two replies and several dozen retweets.

"And best of all," David said. "We were number two in both newscasts last night."

I felt a warm shiver course through me. Most people don't rejoice about coming in second, but considering that Channel Eleven usually ranked fourth out of seven stations, earning the number two slot, even for a night, was real progress.

Susan Andrews smoothed her Trina Turk sheath dress in camera-friendly persimmon and sighed impatiently. I could tell she wasn't happy with the attention this story was getting. After all, it was her steady stream of reports on celebrity marriage breakups, racial slurs spoken by celebrities, celebrity drug use, and celebrity murder trials—along with the occasional story about politicians engaged in extramarital affairs—that dominated our newscasts on a regular basis.

"What I want you to find out—what our viewers want to know—is, who is Good Sam?" David said. "Why is he giving away so much money to so many? Kate, you got any leads?"

"Nothing solid," I admitted.

"I can tell you who he isn't," Alex said, reading from his notebook. "It's not the Red Cross or United Way or any of the major charitable organizations in town. We called a dozen of them this morning, and they all say they're not responsible."

"What if this isn't charitable?" I asked. "What if it's the work of someone who's gaining something from all this attention?"

"Like?" David asked.

"Politicians who want a good reputation, anyone trying to sell anything, anyone who's had negative PR and needs a positive spin—"

"Who *don't* you suspect?" Susan interrupted.

"I think we should look into the connections between the people who received money from Good Sam," I said, ignoring her. "A few of them know each other. Cristina Gomez used to clean Marie Ellis's house. Larry Durham is Dr. K's carpenter. Coincidence or connection?"

"Good thinking," David said, crushing his Dr Pepper can. "Alex, see if you and your team can dig up any connections between these people. Check real estate records, driving records, school records, church records, everything. I want us to be the station to uncloak his identity—"

"Excuse me, Kate." The receptionist interrupted us. "There's a man in the lobby asking to talk to you. He says he's Good Sam."

I glanced at David. Could it be this easy?

The only man in the lobby was young—twenty-three at most—with metal-rimmed glasses and pasty white skin that looked as though it was rarely exposed to the sun.

I walked toward him and extended my hand. "Kate Bradley."

"Tyler Nesbit," he said. Then a smile lifted the corners of his mouth. "Good Sam."

Blame it on my having seen too many movies where the mystery man looks like Gregory Peck or George Clooney, but I imagined Good Sam would be at least thirty-five, with a serious expression and an air of wealth about him. Tyler Nesbit looked like the skinny high school kid who fixes your computer.

The lobby was crowded with school kids on a field-trip tour of the station, so I took him into one of the glass-enclosed conference rooms we used for small meetings. The room afforded a bird's-eye view of our sprawling newsroom below, a perspective that was clearly distracting Tyler.

"That's Susan Andrews, right?" he said, pointing to someone across the room.

I tried to spot Susan on the busy newsroom floor but couldn't. "Could be." I was silent for a long moment. "Are you Good Sam, Tyler?"

He turned from the window and looked me in the eye. "Yes, I am."

I was skeptical, but he had all the details right. Yes, he could have memorized all of it from the news reports, but he had a plausible reason for being Good Sam.

"My parents died when I was fourteen, and my trust fund money recently became available to me," he said. "But it's more than I could ever spend. For weeks I prayed about it. I asked for guidance on how I could serve the Lord with all this money. One night I dreamt I was standing on the doorstep of a beautiful cottage. I had a large bag of money slung over my shoulder, and as I placed the bag on the ground, I felt completely at peace with the world. I took it as a sign of my destiny."

I motioned for him to sit down in one of the black leather chairs. Then I took a seat myself, trying to gather my thoughts in the process. "You think it's your *destiny* to give away five hundred thousand dollars to strangers?"

His voice grew bigger, more confident. "Galatians, chapter six, says, 'Fear not to do good, for whatever you sow, you will also reap; If you sow good, you will also reap good for your reward.'"

"Why are you coming forward now?"

He pushed his glasses to the bridge of his nose. "Because I believe this is my calling now. Through this work I am to spread the word."

"What word is that?" I asked.

"God is coming."

I hesitated a moment, unsure how to handle what he'd said. When you've spent your career reporting on dead bodies, bullet wounds, and burned buildings, you don't get much experience interviewing people about their religious beliefs.

So I dodged. "What's the significance of the number eight on all the bags?"

He leaned forward. "It's not an eight. If you place the bag on its side, you'll see it's the symbol for infinity. It's there because God is infinite."

Although he had the facts straight and his story seemed plausible, something about him didn't ring true. Was it simply that he looked like Doogie Howser with freckles when I was expecting Brad Pitt? Was it his reliance on Scripture and holy words that made me uncomfortable? Or was my reporter's instinct for scams and hoaxes on target?

"I think a lot of people will want to hear your story," I said quietly. "And I think I can make that happen with the top story on the six o'clock news—maybe even get the network to pick it up."

His eyes snapped back to the newsroom below. "Will you be interviewing me down there?"

"Maybe. But the news honchos here and at the network are sticklers about facts. So help me out with some of the details. You gave money to one family so their daughter could go to law school. What was her name again?" I made my question sound informal, as though we were two friends having a casual conversation. But the question was a trap. There was no way he could know the answer from watching the newscasts, because I'd never mentioned the girl's name and as far as I knew, none of the other stations had, either.

He pursed his lips. "I gave the money anonymously. I didn't know anyone's names."

"But you knew their daughter wanted to go to law school." I pressed him. "And you put her name in a letter with the money."

His eyelids fluttered then drifted out again to the scene on the newsroom floor. "Yes, I did. Sorry I can't remember every detail. This whole process has been very demanding . . ."

"Let me see if I can find her name in my notes." I said. I scanned my notes, pretending to look for her name. "I see it here. Elizabeth. Is that right?"

He brightened. "Yes, Elizabeth. That was her name."

"Why did you want Elizabeth to go to law school?"

"Through me I wanted Elizabeth to know that God takes care of everything."

I sat there a moment and let his words hang in the air.

"Tyler, the girl's name was Lauren, not Elizabeth."

He leaned his head back, and his pale blue eyes quickly scanned the ceiling as though he hoped to find an answer there. When he looked back at me, I could see tears had begun to form. "Yes, I know that. I just got confused. You have to believe me."

My voice was a whisper. "How could you possibly forget the name of someone to whom you gave one hundred thousand dollars?"

David Dyal wasn't surprised that Tyler Nesbit was not Good Sam. "Look, we got one. Channel Nine apparently got two fake Good Sams," David said, chugging yet another can of Dr Pepper. "They're all over the Internet—guys claiming to be him."

"Why?" I asked.

He shrugged. "When I covered the O. J. Simpson story, something like thirty people came forward and claimed they did it. A distraction is all it is. Let's get someone who can help develop a psychological portrait of who Good Sam is."

That wouldn't turn out to be an easy task. If Good Sam were a criminal, I would call upon any number of FBI profilers we regularly interviewed to help develop a psychological description. But finding an FBI profiler to work on Good Sam proved to be almost as hard as finding Good Sam himself. Serial killers, child abductors, arsonists, and bombers they understood. None of them had ever encountered a guy giving away more than half a million dollars. A couple of them, however, did give me some advice.

Dr. Ryan Merrill tried to convince me that Good Sam was potentially dangerous. He warned about "icon intimidation," where we automatically assume certain people are harmless because of their behavior.

"The person who appears to be charming and generous," he said, "could very well turn out to be committing heinous crimes."

I admit I often have a skeptical point of view regarding people's motives—it's a hazard of covering breaking news—but even I couldn't wrap my head around the idea that Good Sam might be a dangerous criminal.

Merrill must have sensed my skepticism. "You can't rely on your instincts or intuition, Kate," he said ominously. "They're unreliable in situations like this. Look at it this way. This Good Sam of yours generally leaves no written communication. He wants to leave you in the dark because he knows your imagination will fill in the blanks. You'll create an icon in your mind that likens him to Santa Claus or a fairy godmother or whatever other archetypes of benevolent, generous beings suit you. But that's not who he is."

A chill coursed through my body as I hung up with Ryan Merrill, and the gloomy feeling that hung in the air was so palpable that I left the interview bay and headed straight to the parking lot. Merrill had twenty-eight years with the FBI and had helped capture some of the country's most notorious killers, robbers, and kidnappers. Were those the skills we needed to find Good Sam?

Still, fear sells. And positioning Good Sam as a potential criminal definitely could create a sensation and cause a spike in the ratings. After letting the sun warm my body, however, I knew I couldn't go through with it. Maybe I was stupidly relying on instinct, but I knew Good Sam wasn't a criminal.

Then what kind of person was Good Sam?

Luckily I found Marcus Addison III from the FBI Academy's Behavioral Science Unit. I interviewed him on Skype from his office in Quantico, Virginia. Marcus looked nothing like the handsome FBI profilers they show on TV dramas. With a ragged, scholarly beard, crooked teeth, and beady eyes behind smudged black-rimmed glasses, he clearly spent his time thinking about violent criminals, not his appearance. And he had a completely different take on Good Sam.

"To understand the artist, you must first look at the artwork," he said. "What is he doing? Giving away money. Which tells me he values money a great deal. In fact I wouldn't be surprised if money were his obsession. And don't think he gives secretly in order to be anonymous. The size of the gifts and their ongoing frequency says he wants the attention and is enjoying the media spotlight."

At least someone agrees with me on this point, I thought. "Do you think he wants the attention for some personal gain?" I asked.

Marcus shook his head. "Hard to say. But consider the rush that comes with flipping the television channels and seeing your actions trumpeted, turning on the radio and finding your deeds the focus of so many people's attention. I think he gets tremendous satisfaction from the praise he's getting."

"Why have so many people come forward falsely claiming to be Good Sam?"

He adjusted his tie, but it was still oddly askew. "Think about what Good Sam represents," Marcus said. "He's a mysterious person doing extraordinary good. A lot of attention has been paid to him in the media, and all of it is extremely positive. How often do the news media point their cameras at someone doing good in the world?"

Every TV and radio station in Los Angeles was slammed with phone calls, e-mails, and old-fashioned letters about Good Sam. I thumbed through our latest stack, stunned by the scope of the requests.

"We have less than twelve hours until we lose our home."

"Veteran needs spinal cord surgery."

"My teeth are falling out!"

"I would like to see my mother before she dies."

"Need help buying food for family of seven."

Shop owners throughout the city even got in the act, posting greetings to Good Sam in their windows. "Good Sam: Please Stop In for Mahi-Mahi—on the House!" a sign in a trendy Hollywood bistro read. "Good Sam Welcomed Here," flashed an electronic sign on a men's clothing store in Santa Monica. The bulletin in front of a church in Granada Hills announced the week's sermon: "Any One of Us Could Be the Good Samaritan."

I'd never seen so much attention paid to a local story that wasn't about celebrities, catastrophes, murders, or a combination of all three. And I'd be lying if I said I didn't enjoy all the attention that came with covering such a high-profile story, because I did. I liked the special treatment I got from the news photographers and the respect other reporters gave me. And since my reports were airing on all six newscasts throughout the day, I was getting a lot of airtime.

Meanwhile Alex and a small group of associate producers and interns weren't getting much sleep as they worked around the clock trying to dig up information on Good Sam. After the noon cast, I found Alex leaning back in his chair, surrounded by four half-empty mugs of coffee.

"You guys pull an all-nighter?" I asked.

No answer.

That's when I realized he was asleep. When I was an intern, sleep was the most prized commodity as our excitement about working in a real newsroom energized us to work late into the night and rise early in the morning. I tried to slip away and let him take a power nap, but I ended up tripping over a stack of papers and knocking over his overflowing trash can.

He bolted upright. "I've got a lead," he said. With bleary eyes, he grabbed one of the notebooks on his desk and riffled through the pages. "We've done background checks on the people who received money from Good Sam, looking for anything that might connect them all to each other. Nothing. They attended different colleges or trade schools. They don't go to the same church or synagogues or even shop in the same grocery stores. They're not in similar professions or from the same hometowns. They're different nationalities. It's almost random."

"I thought you said you had a lead," I said, slumping in the chair next to him.

"I said *almost* random. We did a search of the property records, and something interesting came up. It might be a coincidence, but all of them bought their homes from the same seller, Residential Realty Trust, Inc."

"A real estate broker?"

"Not a broker exactly. Residential Realty buys properties, fixes them up, then turns around and sells them."

I thought about this for a moment. "Why would Residential Realty want to give away five hundred thousand dollars?"

Alex chewed on his pencil. "Maybe this is a promotional stunt."

I had to laugh. "Welcome to the dark side. That's what I've been saying all along."

"The thing is, you might actually be right." He set down his notebook. "A little over six months ago, Residential Realty was about to go public with a stock offering that would've made the owners instant millionaires many times over. But they canceled those plans at the last minute—or at least postponed them. One of our sources believes they're in the final stages of taking the company public again. If they are, five hundred thousand dollars would be a small price to pay for the kind of national publicity and attention they're getting."

"So they give the money anonymously, and once the story takes off and becomes a sensation, they swoop in and identify themselves as the generous benefactors."

"You couldn't buy that kind of positive PR for millions of dollars," he added.

I stood. "Who do I call at Residential Realty Trust?"

"I was hoping you'd say that." He ripped a sheet of paper from his notebook and handed it to me. "A guy named Eric Hayes is one of the owners."

"What else do we know about Eric?"

Alex typed a few keystrokes on the computer. "Weird. Looks like he also moonlights as a firefighter. Or maybe it's the other way around, and he moonlights for Residential Realty. The company bio says Mr. Hayes is also a captain in the Los Angeles County Fire Department."

I scanned the bio. "Eric Hayes, captain of the Urban Search and Rescue Team, stationed at Fire Station Eight."

I drew a deep breath. Fire Station Eight.

CHAPTER FOUR

Eric Hayes wasn't on duty at Fire Station Eight, so we looked him up online and then drove to his home, a dark green midcentury house tucked deep in the shade of a rambling oak tree in the Hollywood Hills. This area of the Hills is named The Oaks, not because there are actually very many oak trees, but because all of the street names ended in "Oaks": Green Oaks, Park Oaks, Wild Oaks, Holly Oaks—you get the idea. The house was well kept, yet relatively unassuming. If he was a land baron, he sure hid it well.

Josh readied the camera in the van while I headed to the front door. I glanced once more at the sequence of questions I was planning to ask, slipped the paper in the pocket of my black blazer, then lifted a weathered brass knocker in the shape of a sailboat and knocked.

The door opened, and the first thing I noticed wasn't his face but his legs. Tanned, muscular legs. Legs in shorts even though it was a cold January morning. He wore a navy sweatshirt, and its snug fit didn't hide the athletic body underneath. Most guys with bodies like his usually balanced themselves out by being average in the looks department. But with his thick, sandy-brown hair and full lips, this guy defied the odds. I looked up into light brown eyes shaded by impossibly long eyelashes, and although I make my living talking, I was momentarily speechless.

It took me a few seconds to remember what to do. "I'm Kate Bradley, Channel Eleven News." I extended my hand.

A brief smile crossed his lips. "I know. Eric Hayes."

As he shook my hand, a shock seared through my nervous system. Then I did something I hadn't done since fourth grade when Tommy Watson told the whole class he liked me.

I blushed.

It started as a flicker at the base of my neck and then rushed to my cheeks, so my face felt like I had a third-degree sunburn. I completely forgot what I was going to say next. Everything about him distracted me—from the way he was looking at me to the way he leaned against the doorjamb—shutting off the thinking parts of my brain.

"Which story are you chasing this afternoon?" he asked. "The mosquito-borne virus that's plaguing the Westside or the diaper-wearing chimpanzee that's stopping traffic on Venice Boulevard?"

I smiled. "Guilty of covering those stories in the past."

"Aren't you the one who usually covers breaking news?"

I nodded. "Shootings, sinkholes swallowing homes, mudslides, train collisions—"

"Fires, murders," he said, finishing the list for me. "Viewers like those stories?"

"Fear sells," I said.

His lips were definitely smiling at me now. "Maybe good does, too. It's just harder to find."

I met his gaze for a moment, and my pulse jumped, annoying me.

"As you probably already noticed," he said, "it's all quiet on this street, so what brings you here?"

"I'm here about Good Sam."

"Good who?"

"I guess you haven't been following the news the past twenty-four hours."

He shook his head. "I've been on duty until about an hour ago."

"Over the last few days, five people have found bags containing a hundred thousand dollars in cash on their front porches. We're trying to figure out who this Good Sam is and what his motive is."

"You think someone who's giving away that kind of money has got a *motive*?"

There was a gentleness in Eric's eyes that surprised me. Surely, in his line of work, he'd seen enough bad things that the idea of a truly Good Samaritan seemed as far-fetched as it did to me.

"Not a motive exactly. A reason for giving away so much money to so many."

He shifted his weight to the other foot. "How can I help?"

The words tumbled out of my mouth like I was a cub reporter on her first assignment. "Are you Good Sam?"

"No, but I'd sure like to know why you came all the way here to ask me if I was."

I glanced down at my notes, trying hard not to look at him. "All the canvas bags that contained the money were stamped with the number eight. You're stationed in the Los Angeles County Fire Department's station number eight."

"So are about thirty other firefighters."

I was bombing. Miserably. I hadn't done an interview this poorly since working on my high school newspaper. I exhaled and tried to focus and find my lead.

"All the people who received money from Good Sam bought their homes from Residential Realty Trust, a company you own. We understand the company is about to go public."

Eric shook his head. "I don't own Residential Realty Trust. My brother did."

"Did?"

He shifted his weight to the other leg. "It's a little complicated. Come inside for a minute, and I'll explain."

Inside, his living room was furnished with dark wood furniture that looked sturdy and reliable, like it could withstand anything. Framed oil paintings of sailing ships at sea flanked a cobblestone fireplace, giving the room a warm, comfortable feeling.

"Excuse me a minute. Let me get something that will help clear things up for you," he said, and left the room.

I glanced at the photographs on the mantel. The first captured two young boys in swim shorts hanging in midair as they jumped into a lake. The other was a photograph of Eric and another man standing on the deck of a sailboat under the golden glow of a billowed sail.

"You like sailing?" Eric asked.

As I turned around, I nearly ran straight into him. I lingered there for the briefest of moments, just inches from him, close enough that if I were truly brazen, I could have leaned forward and kissed him.

I didn't, of course—because in that instant, we both jumped back as though we'd touched a hot stove. Until then I didn't believe in attraction at first sight, but there was definitely an immediate, almost magnetic pull developing between us.

"I've never been sailing," I said. "Is that your sailboat?"

"Used to be."

I touched the photograph. "Your brother?"

"Yes."

I studied his brother's face. He was a little shorter than Eric, with a leaner, less athletic build. But judging from the curves of their mouths and their angular jaws, there was no doubt they were brothers.

"Younger or older?" I asked.

"Younger, by fourteen months."

"He's the one who owns Residential Realty Trust?"

The smile faded from his face. "He did. But he passed away six months ago."

"I'm sorry," I murmured. A brief silence passed between us, and neither of us seemed to know how to fill it.

"After he died," Eric continued, "the ownership passed to me and some others, but we sold it last month to a realtor named Paul Henning."

"Is it true that the company plans to go public?"

He shook his head. "Doubt it. My brother had planned to take it public, but he passed away before it could happen. Paul doesn't have quite the same ambition my brother did. Few people do. Here's Paul's card."

His fingertips brushed against mine as he handed me the card. I would have liked to have lingered there a moment longer, but there was a swift knock at the front door and Josh walked in, interrupting the moment. "Brad at the assignment desk just called," he said. "They want a live shot in ten minutes."

I wasn't ready to leave. I had the sinking feeling that once I stepped out of that living room, I'd never see Eric Hayes again.

"Good luck with your story," Eric said.

It was his eyes, I decided, as I headed to the door. It was his eyes, the color of smooth cognac, that were causing all the trouble.

CHAPTER FIVE

By the time I got to the station the next morning, the Good Sam story was all over the network morning newscasts, on talk radio, and in stories across the Internet. Even NPR did a piece about it.

I was baffled at the attention Good Sam was getting. The level of reporting was akin to the coverage of a major natural disaster or a mass shooting, except no one was in danger, at risk, or at large.

I spent so much time poring over all the stories, Facebook posts, and e-mails that I lost track of time and had missed the first ten minutes of the assignment meeting. As I rushed to the Fish Bowl, Alex stopped me.

"There's a psychic in the lobby. She wants to talk to you about Good Sam."

"A psychic?" I said. "Really? That's what this story has come to?"

"She asked to talk with you, Kate, and only you."

"If I miss any more of the meeting, David is sure to assign me to cover some snooze beat. Send her on her way," I said. "But wait—she won't be disappointed, because she's a psychic, so she already saw this coming."

He frowned. "The problem is . . . she's Bonnie's psychic."

I lowered my voice to a half whisper. "Bonnie does not have a psychic."

Bonnie Ungar had joined the station as senior VP of news two months before, with a mandate to bring our ratings from a disappointing fourth place to first. Her take-no-prisoners management style had already cost four news staffers their jobs, and more changes were rumored to be on the way. I wasn't keen to be on her radarscope.

"Actually," Alex said, running his fingers through his hair. "Shondra in security says this woman is Bonnie's psychic—the one she consults every week."

Let me tell you what I think about psychics. They're all frauds. Fakes. They guess bits of information about you and use it to tell you What You Already Know. Then they use that information to make up What You Want to Hear so you'll come back again to learn What You Already Know.

I knew that. But clearly Bonnie Ungar didn't. So for job security's sake, I agreed to meet with the psychic. We set up the interview in one of the recording studios, but I told the tech guy not to record the session. The fastest way to wipe out my credibility would be to record an interview with a psychic.

Melanie Richards wasn't what I'd expected. For one thing she was young. Maybe twenty-five. And pretty. With long, straight dark hair and deep-set eyes. There were no crystals hanging from her neck or wrists, and she wasn't wearing anything that could be described as psychic clothes—just simple slacks and a sweater I recognized from Banana Republic. The only obvious sign that she was a psychic was her pair of Birkenstocks. Mere mortals no longer wore them—certainly not in LA.

"You're from the East Coast, are you?" she said, settling into the mesh chair.

"St. Louis," I said. *One wrong.*

"But you've spent some time there. In school."

"I went to Columbia in New York." *Okay, one right.*

"Your father," Melanie said. "He's an important leader. A congressman or senator."

Another one right. But anyone who googled me could easily find out that my father was Senator Hale Bradley. Besides, why was she telling me about myself when she was supposedly here to talk about Good Sam?

"And something else." She fixed her gaze on a spot about two feet above my head. "Someone in your life wants your attention. But you keep pushing him away."

That was a little close for comfort. Then again that statement could apply to a lot of people.

"You've also just met someone new. Someone you hadn't expected. But you're not sure if he's into you or not."

How could she have known about my meeting Eric Hayes? It was enough to cancel out the one wrong guess.

"Do you understand what I'm talking about?" She continued to look at the spot on the wall.

"Yes." *But is he interested in me?*

Melanie fell silent for a long moment. Then she turned to look straight at me, her deep brown eyes bearing down hard on me. "I came here to tell you about Good Sam. He's in the news everywhere, of course, and last night, I got a reading on him—you might call it a flash of insight—and I know Bonnie would want me to share it with you." She flipped her hair back. "He's in his thirties. He's wealthy, successful. He's doing this to prove something."

"What is he trying to prove?"

She was silent for a long moment. With her eyes closed, I thought maybe she had fallen asleep. "He's not bad. He's done something. Something wrong. And he's trying to undo it."

"And why these people?" I asked.

Melanie scanned the space on the wall, moving her head back and forth slightly, as though she were reading words written right above my head.

Her voice was warm and gentle. "They mean something to someone he loves."

"Why is the number eight stamped on the bags with the money?"

"It's an important number for him. It has significance in his life."

"What's his name?"

She was silent for nearly a minute. "I can't see that," she said finally.

"How do I find him?"

"You must ask the universe to guide you in your quest."

Okay, now she was talking like a psychic. I half expected her to bring out a Ouija board and summon some spirits.

She stood. "That's all."

I stood too, trying to produce an expression that looked like I believed her. At least a little.

"There's something else," Melanie said, fixing her eyes on a spot two feet above my head again. "There's something I should've told you when we began. You will be the one who discovers who Good Sam is."

I didn't know what to make of Melanie Richards. I think she genuinely believed she had psychic powers, but her descriptions of Good Sam's motives were too vague to be helpful. Even so, I had to admit the hairs on the back of my neck rose every time I thought about her prediction.

As much as I wanted to believe I'd be the one to discover Good Sam's identity, I knew Melanie's whole shtick was quackery. I could've made up the same gobbledygook, and I don't have a psychic bone in my body.

By the time I returned to the newsroom, the assignment meeting was long over. There was a box of Godiva chocolates on my desk. I searched for a note or card, but there wasn't one. I figured Jack had sent them, so I dumped them in the trash—which is a shame because I love Godiva chocolates. Just the smell of the crème-brûlée dessert chocolate with layers of butterscotch caramel and vanilla cream makes me feel like I'm eight years old again.

Josh came up to my desk. "I heard you had to interview a psychic. What'd she say?" His eye fell on the candy in my trash can, and the smile faded from his face. "Hey, why'd you throw those chocolates away?"

"I'm on a diet." I lied.

He pulled the box from the trash. "Wish I'd known. They're from me."

"Why?"

"Um, Cathy in Human Resources said it was your birthday tomorrow?"

How could I have forgotten my own birthday? Especially this one. After tomorrow, I'd only have 364 days left in my twenties bank account. Three hundred and sixty-four days until I was no longer a "promising young reporter" and quietly, desperately slipped into "seasoned reporter" status. Another year until thirty.

"Okay, I'm not really on a diet," I said, taking the box from him. "I thought they were from someone else."

"I get it. You thought they were from *him*. The guy you won't talk about."

I nodded. Growing up in a political family had taught me one important lesson. Don't talk about past or current loves, and keep the personal out of the spotlight, because someone might try to use it to gain something from you.

Josh grabbed a chocolate from the box and popped it into his mouth. "Alex says you were meeting with a psychic. What'd she say?"

"She said I'd be the one to discover Good Sam's identity."

"Nut case?"

"Surprisingly normal . . . for a psychic," I admitted.

I looked over and saw Alex coming toward my desk, carrying a small box. "I finally reached Paul Henning, the man who bought Residential Realty from Eric Hayes," he said.

"Any luck?"

He shook his head. "Dead end. He's been out of the country, but he says there's 'no way' Good Sam has anything to do with him or Residential Realty."

I frowned. "Which means we have zero leads."

"If it's any consolation, apparently no one else does, either." He placed the box on my desk. "Oh, and this is for you. The front desk says it was ringing."

"Ringing?"

"You know, like a phone?" Alex said.

"Maybe it's another birthday present," Josh said.

The plain brown box appeared to have been delivered by a local messenger service, but there was no return address. It was also silent. I started to open it, and just as I touched the Bubble Wrap inside, it chimed. I dug through the packing to find a brand-new iPhone.

I answered the call. "Hello?"

"Happy birthday." Jack's warm voice came on the line.

"I thought we agreed that you'd stop sending me things," I snapped.

Hearing my sharp tone, Josh and Alex slunk away from my desk.

"It's your birthday tomorrow, and this is the only way I figured I'd get you to talk to me," Jack drawled.

"We've already said everything that needs to be said."

"What will it take to make you change your mind?"

"I appreciate the thought," I said quietly. "Promise me, Jack. Promise me you won't call me again."

"I really hope you'll change your mind about me. And when you do, I've programmed all my numbers in that phone."

I hung up and dropped the phone into my desk drawer. I ran my fingers through my hair, still shaky from the call. Had I been too tough on him? His gift wasn't inappropriately lavish, unlike his earlier ones. Days after the breakup, he'd sent me a Cartier watch, and for Christmas he'd given me a David Yurman necklace, which I'm pretty sure retailed for five thousand dollars. Maybe I should've viewed the phone as a kind of olive branch.

The phone on my desk rang, startling me. I grabbed the receiver. "I thought we agreed you'd stop calling."

"We did?" I heard a man's voice say. But it wasn't Jack.

"I'm sorry. Who's this?" I asked.

"Eric Hayes. Sounds like you get some pretty annoying calls."

"More so lately." I wasn't sure what else to say. But I did know I should say something witty or charming so he wouldn't know how happy I was to hear his voice, calm and steady, on the other end of the phone. "I just met with a psychic who says I'm going to figure out who Good Sam is. Are you calling to make this easy and confess to being him?" I hope I sounded casual, not like I was trying too hard.

A distorted voice came over a loudspeaker on his end, followed by a series of tones.

"Sorry, but I've got to run. Could we meet at Sam's Bagels, the one around the corner from Channel Eleven? How about seven tomorrow morning?"

I felt the air back up in my lungs. Was this a kind of date? Or was he asking to meet me because I was a reporter at Channel Eleven? Was this about Good Sam?

"Sam's Bagels at seven," I repeated.

CHAPTER SIX

The next morning I spent more time than usual getting ready. Putting my hair in rollers to give it extra volume. Applying a little more blush than usual. I tried on three outfits before settling on a raisin-brown blazer with pencil skirt and delicate gold necklace. As I glanced one final time in the car mirror, I kicked myself for going overboard. This wasn't a date. It was breakfast at a bagel shop.

It had been six months since I'd broken it off with Jack, and I hadn't dated anyone since then. A while back, Teri had tried to set me up on a date with a guy she knew from the marketing department at Hallmark Channel, but even though he looked fun in his Facebook photo, I turned down the date. I wasn't ready.

But I was attracted to Eric—more than I wanted to admit—and couldn't deny the extra lift in my step as I made my way into Sam's Bagels. Was I ready now?

Sam's is a hole-in-the-wall shop with the best bagels in town. The secret recipe is known only by Sam and his two sons, Perry and Harold. Rumor has it, the secret is in the perfect pH and mineral content of the water used to boil the bagels, but I suspect the real secret is in the schmear—the pounds of cream cheese they pile on.

There was a line out the door for takeout and a shorter line for the handful of tables they had in the back of the restaurant. Eric had already secured one of the red vinyl booths that probably had been there since Watergate. He was dressed in a pressed blue fire department uniform, his hair slightly damp. Damn, he was good-looking. He smiled at me, and my heart did that same flip-flopping thing it had done the first time I met him.

"You made it," he said warmly, and handed me a bagel wrapped in waxed paper. "Toasted bagel with everything. Plain cream cheese."

I tilted my head. "How did you know how I like my—"

He pushed a cup across the table. "Coffee. Black. Definitely caffeinated. One sugar. No artificial sweetener."

"How did you—"

"The cameraman who was with you the day I met you—his name is Josh, right?—was standing in front of me in line a few minutes ago. I told him I was meeting you for breakfast, and he gave me your life story."

"My life story?"

"The parts he could tell in thirty seconds. He told me what you eat for breakfast, said your favorite snack is spicy almonds that you have shipped from Texas, and that you jog around Lake Hollywood Reservoir every morning."

"Run." I corrected myself. "Not jog."

"I swim every morning at the pool by the reservoir. Ever go inside to swim, or are you strictly a runner?"

"Strictly a runner. I don't swim."

"Never?"

"Actually I almost drowned last month," I said, then wished I hadn't because, of course, he was going to ask for details. And we'd barely been there two minutes.

He leaned forward. "Drowned? Where?"

Three weeks later I still remembered every detail of that day. The summery smell of the 55-SPF sunscreen. The warm, wet sand squishing between my toes. None of that foretold the danger to come.

"In Mexico," I said, my voice wavering. "I'd gone there with a friend to celebrate her thirtieth birthday. She had overdone it on the celebrating part and slept in one morning, so I went to the beach alone. The hotel was on a stretch of beach lined with eco-resorts so there weren't any lifeguards." I took a gulp of coffee, for fortitude. "I'm not a good swimmer—I didn't learn how to swim until late in high school—so I'm pretty cautious around water. But the water was warm, the sun was shining high in the sky, and I kind of lost track of things and ventured out farther than I'd meant to. Out of nowhere a huge wave rose up and knocked me over. In a flash it dragged me out to where I couldn't touch the bottom anymore."

"A rip current," he said quietly.

I swallowed the lump in my throat. I hadn't told anyone about this before. Not even Teri. Talking about it freshened the memories and made me feel strangely wobbly, as though it were all happening again. "Enough about my terror in Mexico," I said, trying to lighten the mood.

"How long were you stuck in the riptide?"

I reached for my coffee and took another sip. "I'm not sure. It seemed like hours, but it was probably less than fifteen minutes. I lost track of time. The waves kept pulling me under. Then I'd come up for a few minutes and try to swim toward land. But I wasn't getting anywhere. I was just pulled farther out to sea."

"Did you know it was a riptide?"

"At first I didn't. I screamed for help several times, but my voice sounded so strangled, so small, that it actually made me panic and confused about what to do."

"Did anyone on the beach come to help?"

I didn't want to say anything more. This was the part of the story that was still hard to fathom. I wanted to talk about something easier.

Eric seemed to read my mind. "They didn't, did they?" He moved his hand an inch toward mine, but then seemed to think better of it and stopped. "Most people in situations like that don't help. They don't know what to do."

I took a deep breath and tried to steady my nerves. "Each time I came up for air, I looked at the shore, and I saw people looking in my direction, but no one came toward me. Dozens of people were onshore, and no one did anything . . ." I trailed off. In the silence, I felt his eyes upon me.

"But you're here today, so somehow you managed to get out. Even though you don't know how to swim very well. How?"

The words came more easily now. "I began to swim—or my weak version of it—parallel to shore. I'd be able to move a foot or two before a wave would crest over me and bring me under again. Eventually one of the hotel's security guards pulled me out. By the time he got to me, I was five hundred feet from shore and barely conscious."

"Something like that can be very hard to shake," he said. "It's going to take time to get over it." He said it as though he had been there. As though he understood. In that moment I felt oddly connected with him, as if I'd known him for a very long time.

"So what's your story?" I asked, trying to change the subject. "Captain of the Urban Search and Rescue Team and swift-water rescue expert. Were you the kid who always wanted to be a firefighter when he grew up?"

A waiter came by and refilled our coffee cups. "Actually I wanted to be a TV journalist when I grew up."

"You're joking, right?"

"Dead serious. I thought Peter Jennings's job looked pretty exciting—traveling the world, covering big news events."

"Good thing you got some sense and did something with your life," I said with a smile. "What changed your mind?"

"Seventh grade. Sam Moretti," he said without missing a beat. "There was a ditch beneath a concrete-lined drainage channel in front of our house. A bunch of us guys in the neighborhood played there all the time, using it as a kind of foxhole. One afternoon the drainage pipe collapsed and trapped Sam Moretti beneath it. The guys from the fire department came, and for two hours we watched these six guys risk their lives to pull him to safety. I knew then that I wanted to be a part of something like that."

"It has to be hard," I said, "putting your life on the line for other people."

He shrugged. "I like knowing that every day I'm helping to make things better."

Anyone else saying those words would've sounded pretentious or hopelessly naive. But the way Eric said it, straightforward and unrehearsed, left no doubt that he was neither.

He took a slug of his coffee. "I'm really glad you came today," he said. "I wasn't sure you'd show once you knew I wasn't the Good Sam you're looking for."

I bit into my bagel. "We haven't completely ruled you out as a suspect."

"So I'm still a suspect?"

"Do you have an alibi, Captain Hayes?" I was flirting with him now, enjoying his gaze and the smile on his lips.

"Actually I do." He pulled out an iPad and pointed to one of the headlines on the *LA Times* website.

It read, "Good Sam Still Giving."

"'Neither rain nor floods nor inclement weather kept Good Sam from his appointed rounds yesterday,'" he read aloud. "'Just after 4:00 p.m. on Wednesday, Pacific Palisades resident Charles DeVault heard a rustling noise at his front door and was surprised to find a canvas bag containing one hundred thousand dollars in cash on his front porch. The bag was stamped with a lopsided number eight.' Where was I around four o'clock Wednesday afternoon when Charles DeVault got his money?" Eric asked.

I searched my memory for what I was doing Wednesday afternoon and came up blank. "I don't know."

"Actually you do. Because I was with you. And your cameraman." He cradled the coffee mug in his hands and leaned back in his seat. "That's when we first met. Now that's pretty convincing proof, isn't it?"

I grinned. "That's some fairly good evidence, but you should know I'm never one hundred percent convinced about anything."

He glanced back at his iPad. "Here's more then. The article goes on to mention three other people who received one hundred thousand dollars that day—Maria Villegas, Peter Caruso, and Jocelyn Frierson. All of them say they found a bag stamped with the number eight on their front porch sometime between four and six o'clock, the same time I was meeting with you."

He handed me the iPad, and I scanned the *Times* article. With a sinking feeling, I realized Channel Eleven had not known about—much less reported on—a single one of these Good Sam recipients.

"Have you considered the idea that there might be a copycat Good Sam out there?" he said. "Look at how many people reported that they received a hundred thousand dollars that day. Four people in one day. And unlike the first few, who were spread out throughout the county, these new ones are all clustered on one area of the map—Pacific Palisades, Manhattan Beach, El Segundo, and Venice."

"You've got a great eye," I said, picking up my phone. "Even the *Times* didn't spot the pattern you're talking about. Mind if I call the newsroom about this?"

"Now are you convinced I'm not him?"

"I don't know." I smiled. "Maybe if we kept watch over you one night and made sure you didn't go anywhere."

"I might like that." His lips parted in a slight grin. "Your keeping watch over me one night."

His words threw me off balance. Our eyes met, and neither of us said a word. The moment that enveloped us drowned out the hissing of the coffee machines, muffled the clatter of plates and silverware, and silenced the conversations around us.

His cell phone vibrated then, skittering on the tabletop and breaking the spell. He glanced at it and frowned. "Captain Hayes," he answered. I watched him listen for a moment and then respond. "I'll be en route in a few minutes." He ended the call and met my gaze. "I'm really sorry to jump like this," he said, tossing a few bills on the table. "There's a warehouse fire downtown. Some people are missing, so we have to do a search operation."

"I understand."

He started to leave, but then turned around. "I almost forgot. Happy Birthday."

"How did you—"

"Your cameraman told me that, too. Can we do this again . . . maybe celebrate your birthday?"

I smiled, more broadly than I'd intended.

David Dyal was the only person in the Fish Bowl when I arrived for the assignment meeting that morning. He was dressed in his usual pinstripe shirt—today it was blue and white—and khaki pants with brown suede suspenders. He sat at the head of the empty conference table, reading the newspaper on his iPad.

"Am I early?" I asked.

"Close the door," he said without looking up. He was massaging his right ear.

You know you're in trouble when David Dyal rubs his ear. If he's bored, he runs his fingers through his hair. If a story is mildly interesting, he brushes his hand back and forth across his chin as he listens. But when he's unhappy or under pressure, he rubs his right ear. Sometimes with a pencil. Sometimes with his hand. Always his right ear.

I closed the door and sat down in the chair next to him. "What's going on?"

"Any idea how this happened?" he asked. He waved the *Times* article about Good Sam at me. "How they managed to score exclusive interviews with four people who received a hundred thousand dollars and we didn't even report it?" I opened my mouth to answer, but he cut me off. "You know, your years on the Bummer Beat haven't exactly prepared you for a story like this, Kate." His words fell like crushing weights. "The networks are putting their best reporters out there to cover it. I think you're in way over your head on this one."

"Is this supposed to be a pep talk? Because if it is, I'm not feeling—"

"Look, Bonnie is furious about this. She wants to bring on someone with a higher profile."

"I don't—"

"She wants Susan Andrews," he said flatly.

Anger lit my nerves. "She wants Susan to take over *my* story?" Before David could answer, I put up my hand to stop him. "I broke this one. I miss this development and you guys want to give the assignment to Susan?"

"Kate," he said with a sigh. From his tone, I knew a lecture was heading my way. "You know how it works. This story is big. Really big. Bonnie wants the most recognized face—the one with the highest profile—on this. It's an insurance policy. If we fail and another station finds Good Sam before we do or nabs better ratings than we do, we can say we put our best talent out there. It won't be our fault. But if we put you out there and you fail, everyone will question why we put the Bummer Beat reporter on one of the biggest stories of the year."

I wanted to shout at him or at least kick a trash can or toss a swear word around. But I knew better. The last reporter who threw a tantrum about an assignment ended up covering the Department of Public Works' sediment removal projects for two weeks straight.

"So I don't have any say in this." My voice sounded far away, even to me. "You and Bonnie are taking me off the story. For no reason."

"I'm saying you should focus your energies on your strengths, Kate—breaking news. And if you're tired of that, maybe it's time you reconsidered the political beat."

It was my turn to sigh. "We've been through this before. I don't want to cover the political beat."

He leaned back in his chair, and for the first time, he looked at me. "I've always thought that was a mistake, you know. Your father's connections could get you access to just about every policymaker in the country. It could propel you to becoming one of the top political pundits on TV news someday."

"A reporter is always looking for a story, right? Well, I already know what stories I'd find on the political beat. Hypocrisy, bribery, dishonesty. Philandering politicians. Besides, I don't want to be a pundit. I want to report the news."

David wasn't listening. In fact he was looking at something on his phone. "Thanks for taking this so well, Kate."

I must have been giving an award-winning performance in there, because I wasn't taking it well at all. Anger and disappointment flushed my face. My hands were clenched so tight my knuckles had turned white.

The psychic had been wrong. I wasn't going to find Good Sam. But that wasn't what was bothering me; I never expected her to be right. I only *wanted* her to be right.

I had forged a strange connection to the Good Sam story. Call it reporter's intuition or gut instincts or plain old self-deception, but I actually felt I was on a path to discovering who Good Sam was—even though I didn't have any solid leads.

Riding on that anger, I marched out of the Fish Bowl. Some birthday this turned out to be. I got twenty steps away and then stopped. I considered going back to demand that he put me back on Good Sam. But then I lost my resolve, and it was all I could do to make my way to my desk.

A deafening boom startled me awake the next morning. I shot straight up in bed, instantly alert, trying to identify the source. The last time I'd heard a mammoth sound like that, a meth lab had exploded in a Hollywood apartment building six blocks away. I'd been the first reporter on the scene that night, the first to break the story at the top of our eleven o'clock newscast. Would it be too much to hope for another meth-lab explosion?

A flash of light pierced the darkness. Then I heard the drumming sound of rain pelting the roof. I groaned and burrowed under the covers.

I hate it when it rains in Los Angeles. I don't own a real raincoat or boots, and I never can remember where I put any of the three umbrellas I own. And no one looks good in the rain, especially TV reporters in station-issued storm gear that adds twenty pounds.

On the plus side, rain brought with it a whole slew of great story possibilities. Mudslides in the mountains and canyons. Flooding in the water-control channels. Hubcap-deep water. Car collisions. Stalled traffic on the freeways. Power outages. Stories that got plenty of airtime.

I tried to convince myself that the extra airtime would make up for my being ripped from the Good Sam story, but it wasn't working. I was still smarting from the offense and considered making my case directly to Bonnie Ungar. But so far everyone who had gone into her office to complain about anything came out unemployed.

Okay, maybe she wasn't actually that trigger-happy, but I figured I'd wait a bit, allow Susan Andrews to disappoint them, too, then make my case.

I hurried through a two-minute shower, threw on some wrinkle-resistant pants, grabbed the station-issued rain jacket and matching blue umbrella, and hurried out the door. Los Angeles is utter chaos when it rains. The streets turn into a real-life version of bumper cars where vehicles skid, spin, and slam into each other the minute the rain hits the pavement. Some pundits have theorized that because it rains so infrequently, oil and grime collect on the freeways, making them unusually slick. I suspect the real reason is that Los Angeles drivers spend so much time in their cars driving under blue skies and sunshine that we don't think of driving as an activity that requires attention, skill, and, yes, caution.

My commute to the station took fifteen minutes longer than usual, but I was grateful that I had arrived without getting stuck in standstill traffic or caught in a fender bender.

"We got team coverage today, folks," David Dyal said, rushing into the assignment meeting. "Weather Service says this storm is going to dump three inches in the next twenty-four hours. I need three of you on 'Storm Watch.' Charles, Orange County. Ted, you cover Inland Empire and the Valley." He motioned to me with his Dr Pepper can. "Kate, you've got Malibu and the beach communities."

I smiled. Even the possibility of a mudslide in any of the beach communities was a guarantee of airtime. Lots of it. And not just in Los Angeles. Network news. Viewers around the country can't get enough of watching nature in all its unpredictable glory putting multimillion-dollar homes in harm's way.

There were no reports yet of mudslides or accidents in Malibu, but Josh and I headed that way so we'd be there if any news broke. Not that I was wishing tragedy upon anyone, but I did hope something newsworthy would happen to make the trip worthwhile. Otherwise I'd have to do a dreaded "reaction story," which would require standing in the downpour and interviewing drivers about how the rain was ruining their commute.

We hadn't been on the road very long before David's voice crackled over the two-way radio. "A boy has fallen in the river in Malibu Canyon. How fast can you get there?"

"Be there in five," Josh answered.

My throat constricted. "Is the fire department on the scene?"

"They are, but they can't get to him," David said. "Chopper Eleven is on its way. Feed it live when you get there."

I couldn't move. Although adrenaline sped through my veins, I had a bad feeling about this story.

Stan McCort, the reporter in Chopper Eleven, had a bird's-eye view of the canyon. "Looks like the fire department's got the canyon blocked off," he said. "You won't be able to get a clear shot."

"What about the turnout on Mountain Pass? Can I get a shot from there?" Josh called out.

"Yeah, if you can find it in this downpour."

Josh knew exactly where it was. I'm pretty sure he had a photographic memory of just about every square mile of Los Angeles County. The narrow mountain roads were slick with rain, but he drove with confidence, smoothly navigating the sharp curves and avoiding the rocks and debris that had tumbled onto the road.

"The boy's moving downstream in your direction," Stan shouted over the radio.

Josh slammed on the brakes, and we slid three feet before pulling to a stop at a narrow turnout. With practiced calm, he jumped out of the van to raise the antenna that would beam our signal back to the station. I put on the earpiece that would connect me to Stan and the control room at the station, zipped up my station-issued storm gear, and opened the door. A strong wet gust yanked it out of my hand, drenching me from head to toe in chilly rain.

"The fire department has deployed multiple units along the stream but hasn't been able to intercept the boy," Stan said. "He's moving fast. Wearing a white T-shirt, Kate."

I peered over the rim of the canyon into the swirling waters four hundred feet below and felt my head spin. I backed away and leaned against the side of the van.

"You all right?" Josh shouted, hoisting the camera onto his shoulder and aiming it into the canyon.

I signaled him with a thumbs-up. But I wasn't okay. The memories stabbed at me like splinters of glass. I tried to catch my breath. I was drowning again, but this time in slow motion. My body, leaden and heavy, sunk into the milky depths. I felt the bone-chilling cold of the water, the scrape of the rocks and debris against my skin, the searing pain in my lungs as I was dragged deep into the turbid darkness.

"Coming to you live in four minutes, Kate," Craig from the control room said in my earpiece.

"Okay," I replied, surprised at the steadiness of my voice.

"Stan and Josh," Craig continued. "The rain is making it a little fuzzy but we've got picture from both of you. We're recording and will roll the footage hot when we come to Kate live in four."

From around the bend, a fire department helicopter buzzed downstream carrying a man suspended from a cable about forty feet below the helicopter. I wasn't sure what they were doing until I saw a white flash in the water.

The boy.

The helicopter chased the boy downstream, matching his speed. The rescuer on the wire grabbed for him, but the current was strong and pulled the boy away. The helicopter attempted a second pass, but when the rescuer reached for the boy this time, the child went under. The helicopter lifted up, pulling the rescuer thirty feet into the air, and hovered.

"The Malibu Tunnel is about five hundred yards downstream," Stan shouted. "If they don't get him before then, he's in for a very bumpy ride."

Suddenly the rescuer detached himself from the rope and plunged thirty feet into the rushing whitewater below. He swam around the rocks and eddies, quickly covering the territory where the boy was last seen, then dove underneath. Seconds ticked by. Every nerve in my body was on edge. With each passing moment, the chances of this boy surviving were slipping away.

"Anyone see the rescuer?" Josh asked, his camera trained on the rushing water.

I scanned the rugged terrain with my binoculars, but all I could see was the water rushing over the rocks and chaparral, and the helicopter hovering above the swollen stream. The rescuer had been gone so long that I'd lost track of where he'd last been.

"Can't see anything from here," Stan said, his voice solemn.

The sky darkened, and the rain began to blow sideways. I scanned the water again, praying for my eyes to glimpse anything that might suggest the rescuer and the boy were alive.

"Looks like the rescuer's down," Stan said. "They're calling for backup."

It was a good thing we weren't on-air because the situation had taken an abrupt, somber turn that can be difficult to report on live. Words fail you in moments like these. Even though I'd reported on many failed rescues, it's never easy telling the tragic story of lost lives, especially young ones.

Suddenly the rescuer popped straight out of the water, his arms wrapped firmly around the boy. I loosened my death grip on the handle of my umbrella. As I watched the helicopter swoop over them, tears warmed my eyes. A mixture of exhilaration and awe swept over me. This was why I covered the Bummer Beat—for the moment when a life is saved, a crisis is averted, and good triumphs.

"The boy's not moving," Stan said in a hushed whisper.

I'd been too optimistic. I peered through my binoculars and held my breath, afraid of what I might see. The boy, no more than seven years old, didn't move as the rescuer placed a strap around his chest and clipped the strap to the cable.

With the rescuer and boy still attached to the line below, the helicopter took off up the canyon. In my binoculars, I saw the rescuer, hanging a hundred feet above the water, perform CPR on the boy's limp body. I struggled not to cry, but tears burned at the corners of my eyes.

The helicopter ascended through the steep canyon, clearing treetops and rock outcroppings, with the rescuer and boy spinning beneath it. That's when I saw the set of high-tension wires draped from rim to rim across the canyon about five hundred feet from the ground. Like a silent enemy, they threatened to snag the rescuer and the boy, dangling like a tetherball below the helicopter.

The helicopter inched closer and closer to the wires. In the thick gray air and fog, I wondered whether the pilot could see the thin lines. Then the helicopter pitched upward several hundred feet, pulling the rescuer and the boy with it, deftly clearing the wires.

"Damn," Josh said with a choke in his voice.

"Kate," Craig said through my earpiece, "coming to you in sixty. Ready?"

"Ready." The sound of my voice, calm and assured, surprised me again.

"He's got a pulse," Craig said. "We've got Urban Search and Rescue on the line. They say the boy's got a pulse again."

There was an excited whoop in my earpiece that sounded like it came from Stan. Josh rushed over, slapped a microphone into my hand,

and trained his camera on me. I ran my fingers through my hair in a futile attempt to correct the mess the rain had made, then adjusted my earpiece, listening for the "Breaking News" intro and waiting for my cue from the anchor, Mark Edwards.

"Live in Malibu Canyon, Channel Eleven's Kate Bradley is on the scene of the dramatic rescue of a young boy," Mark announced.

I don't remember exactly what I said after that. All I know was that the words came out effortlessly. While the station rolled the dramatic footage, I stepped away from reciting the facts and told viewers about the awe all of us on the Channel Eleven crew felt as this heroic fire-fighter plunged in the rushing water to rescue the young boy, about the rescuer's unwavering courage and determination to find the boy even as the storm worsened and his own life was at risk, and about the daring maneuver and swift action that defied the odds and brought the young boy to safety.

"You didn't look so great when we first got there, Kate, but you nailed that live report," Josh said as we sped toward the hospital to see whether we could nab an interview with someone from the fire department or the victim's family.

"Thanks." I managed to say.

Two cups of the rocket fuel sludge he'd brought in his thermos was enough to keep me humming for days. Even so, I couldn't get warm. I shivered into the fleece blanket we had borrowed from the station's emergency survival kit. It could've been a hundred degrees in the news van, and I still would have been cold. But it wasn't just the downpour that had done me in. It was the memory of the water closing in on me, squeezing the life out of me.

After my near drowning, I'd considered moving someplace where there was no water. Like the Sahara desert—three and a half million square miles without water. Or maybe Arica, in northern Chile, which has the lowest rainfall in the world. Unfortunately, those places don't employ very many TV news reporters.

A three-car pileup on the 10 freeway had traffic backed up for miles, but that didn't slow us down. Josh zipped down narrow side streets, drove the wrong way down several one-way alleys, and piloted the vehicle through a mini-mall parking lot as though he were driving a Porsche Boxster, not a Ford panel van loaded down with remote broadcast equipment.

"I'm from Channel Eleven," I said to the emergency room technician at UCLA Medical Center. "What can you tell us about the condition of the boy caught in Malibu Canyon?"

"I can't release any information," she said with robotic efficiency.

A man with a gash on his forehead shifted impatiently in the line behind me.

"Has he regained consciousness?"

Her eyes didn't leave her computer screen. "I don't have that information."

"Are any of the rescue personnel from the scene still here?" I pressed.

"You'll have to check outside. I can't help you."

The security guard, built like a linebacker for the New England Patriots, shot me a look that was supposed to persuade me to move on. It wasn't working. "Is there a doctor—anyone—who can tell me about the boy's condition?"

"Not at this time. Now please step aside."

I checked the sidewalks in front of the ER entranceway, but there was no sign of the fire department—just a gaggle of TV cameramen, field producers, and reporters trying to nab the same story.

"There he is," one of the reporters said, pointing toward the parking lot. "That's the guy who pulled the boy out."

I hadn't expected to come face-to-face with the rescuer. I would have settled for an emergency room doctor or a firefighter on the scene.

But interviewing the actual rescuer would be a big coup. I raced with the pack of reporters toward the figure in the parking lot. At first his back was to us, but the clamor from the reporters must have caught his attention, and he turned around.

It was Eric Hayes. His hair was wet and tousled, and he was still wearing the black-and-yellow dry suit I had seen in the water. His eyes looked tired, but there was another emotion that registered across his face. Relief perhaps. Satisfaction.

Anna Hernandez, the guerrilla reporter from Channel Four, shoved a microphone in his face. "Are you the firefighter who rescued the boy in Malibu Canyon?"

He nodded.

"What can you tell us about the boy's condition?"

"He's in critical but stable condition."

"Tell us about the rescue operation."

Eric took a step back. "I'm sorry, everyone, but I'm not doing interviews."

Jennifer Hastings, the breaking-news reporter from Channel Two, tried a different tactic. "Viewers really should hear your story. They need to understand what went through your mind during this dramatic rescue."

I detected a hint of fear in Eric's eyes. Whitewater rapids clearly didn't faze him, but the idea of a TV interview seemed to be getting under his skin. "Our communications officer will be out here shortly to take your questions."

He turned and headed toward the fire truck in the back of the parking lot. A few of the reporters were frowning, but most were already on their cell phones, trying to get more information.

"Eric?" I called out to him.

Anna whirled around to look at me, clearly eager to swoop in if I was able to get the rescuer to turn around.

Eric turned, and when he saw me, he smiled. "Kate."

I didn't hide my admiration. "All my years covering this beat, and I've never seen anything like what you did today," I said, walking toward him.

He looked away, as though he was uncomfortable with my compliment. "It's what we train for."

"Is the boy okay?" I asked.

"You know what?" he said, his eyes brightening. "They think he's going to be all right." I was surprised when he casually slung his arm around my shoulder. "We'd better keep walking toward the truck, acting like we're having a private conversation," he said conspiratorially. "Or your reporter friends are going to accost me again."

"They're not very strong. I think you could fight them off," I said. Could he tell how much I liked the feel of his arm around my shoulder?

He turned to look at me. "Aren't you going to ask me for an interview?"

"I think I heard you say back there that you don't do interviews."

"And you accepted that? Funny. I've seen you on the news, Kate. I don't think you accept no from anyone."

His smile deepened, and I felt genuine warmth coming from him. We were getting close to the fire truck, and I had the feeling he was going to drop his arm at any moment.

"Okay, then," I said. "Any chance of an interview, Captain Hayes? Two minutes tops. Completely pain-free."

I touched my hand to his arm. It was a reflex action, something I often did to anchor nervous interviewees in the midst of all the lights and cameras and commotion. Eric glanced at my hand on his arm and then back at me. I took a deep, steadying breath. I was here to get a story, remember? Not fall for a brave rescuer.

"Okay," he said. "But can we do the interview at the fire station? I have something for you there."

"You have something for *me* there?" I asked. "What is it?"

He dropped his arm from my shoulders and hopped into the passenger seat of the idling fire truck. "Guess you'll have to go there and find out."

⌇

I sat in the car for five minutes after I reached the fire station in West Los Angeles. Josh had been called to cover a "show-and-tell"—brief footage of a three-car pileup on the rain-slicked Pacific Coast Highway. Meanwhile another cameraman was on his way for my interview with Eric and was supposed to get here within five minutes.

In TV news time, five minutes can be an eternity. Someone else can scoop us on the story in that time frame, which means we can't promote "exclusive" or "for the first time" coverage.

I checked my makeup in the mirror, rubbed my sweaty palms together until they were bone-dry, brushed the lint off my lavender cardigan, and checked my makeup again. My still-damp hair was a little flatter than usual but looked surprisingly okay for having been stuck in a rainstorm.

Three Altoids later, I finally mustered the nerve to get out of the car and walk to the front door of Los Angeles County Fire Department Station Eight. I'd been less nervous interviewing the governor of California.

My breath hitched when Eric opened the door. He was dressed now in a pair of faded blue jeans and a white cotton shirt, open at the neck. His easy, confident stance was distracting me from my mission.

"Come on in," he said, ushering me into the building. "Where would you like to do the interview?"

"In the garage with the fire truck as a backdrop would be good. Thanks for agreeing to do this."

I followed him down a long corridor toward the garage. Before opening the door, he paused and looked at me. "What would you say if I told you that agreeing to the interview was just a convenient excuse to see you again?"

I felt my cheeks grow hot. I didn't know what to say because I didn't want him to know how glad I was to see him again, too. I tried not to let on what I was thinking. "You say that now," I said lightly, "but you might regret it after I'm done interviewing you."

"I doubt that," he said.

As he pushed open a large door that led to the vehicle holding area, I noticed the faint scar that ran the length of his right forearm.

"How did you get that?" I asked, pointing to the scar.

He glanced at his arm and shrugged. "Hazards of the search-and-rescue business. We all have them. This one isn't that bad, considering."

We stepped into the cool garage, where one of the freshly washed fire trucks stood. "Considering what?"

"You ask a lot of questions, don't you?" he said with an appreciative grin.

I met his smile with one of my own. "What makes you say that?"

"Did you know that in Russia they actually have a word for a person who asks too many questions? I think they call them *pochemuchka*. I learned that from a Russian crew member."

"I may be a *pochemuchka*, but if you think that little factoid is going to distract me from my question, it won't work," I said. "Now, will you tell me how you got that scar?"

He stretched the stiffness from his body. "A couple of years ago a boy and his father were rappelling down a shaft at Black Jack Mine. The boy was able to get out, but his father fell and got wedged in a narrow part of the shaft about two hundred feet down. By the time we arrived, the man was slipping in and out of consciousness, so they lowered me down on a rope headfirst to pull him out. When I went to tie a rope around him, my arm scraped across a metal pin that was sticking out the side of the shaft. It sliced my arm almost to the bone."

I winced. "That had to hurt."

"I didn't feel any pain until I got out of the mineshaft much later. I was focused only on getting him out of there. Once you see the person and talk to them, you realize the gravity of the situation and nothing—not even mind-numbing pain—stops you from getting them to safety."

"Did you get him out?"

Eric let out a long breath. "I didn't think I could because he was heavy—close to three hundred pounds—and the way he was positioned, it would take the strength of at least two men to unwedge him. But there was no way two of us would fit in that narrow shaft, so we were beginning to run out of options. Then he opened his eyes and said, 'I'm not going to make it, am I?' I told him everything would be okay and gave him a flashlight to hold, and then I got him out of there." He said it plainly, as though it was commonplace to be in such a situation. But his was the face many saw when they thought they were going to die. It was his comforting words, his gestures of caring and feats of courage that would carry them from the brink of death. Didn't he see he was extraordinary?

"But your arm was cut to the bone and bleeding. Why didn't they put someone else in your place?"

"My crew wanted to take me out because I'd been hanging upside down for so long. They didn't even know I was injured. But I wasn't ready to let this one go, so I asked for another five minutes. And somehow—I don't know how exactly—I managed to unwedge him and pull him out."

"And he ended up okay?"

"You really do ask a lot of questions."

I smiled. "We journalists have to take everything apart and dissect it in order to understand it. We can't all be superheroes like you."

His eyes drifted to a spot over my shoulder. "I'm no superhero. I'm just a guy doing a job."

"A job where you put your life in danger for people you don't know."

"A lot of things must seem dangerous to someone who makes her living talking to a camera," he said, teasing.

I plastered a mock frown on my face. "You make me sound like I'm some kind of bubblehead reporter."

Eric raised his eyes to meet mine. "I think you're anything but."

I was aware of how close we were standing, the way his body angled toward mine, the curve of his jaw as he smiled at me. I noticed the playful glint in his eyes and wondered whether he had any idea what I was thinking. I had the feeling he did, which made me nervous.

"Have your eyes always been green?" I asked, hoping my question would cover my nervousness.

"Now that's a line no one's ever used on me before," he said, still smiling.

"Really," I protested, and felt my cheeks flush red. Why isn't there a cure for blushing? "When I looked at them before, I thought they were brown."

"They're gray. They look different depending on the light."

He was right, of course. They were gray with flecks of brown and green.

He leaned closer to me, and the space between us vibrated with tension and possibility.

"Sorry I'm late," Drake, the Channel Eleven cameraman, said, interrupting the moment as he lumbered in with the camera and sound equipment.

Eric was a natural in front of the camera. His voice shook a little at first, but as the seconds ticked by, he seemed to forget the camera and relaxed into his answers.

I, on the other hand, couldn't get used to looking at him. For all his good looks, he had a commanding authority and a genuine, no-nonsense way of speaking.

"That part of Malibu Canyon is brimming with sharp rocks and debris," I said. "How did you find the boy in all that?"

"I concentrated on the water, not the boy," he said. "If you want to defeat the water, you have to think like it—how it's flowing, where its hiding places are, what its weaknesses are. Once I got a feel for what the water was doing, I found the boy wedged between a rock and a tree, about four feet beneath the surface."

"You put yourself in extraordinary jeopardy," I said. "You disconnected from the tether and jumped thirty feet into rapid water, a maneuver some would say was risky and dangerous. Why?"

He shrugged as if what he had done was completely ordinary. "It's part of the job. But what looks daring and reckless really is a carefully thought-out plan that we've trained for before. I knew what I was risking and what I had to do to save the boy. And I knew that if we did it right, he'd still be walking around tomorrow."

Minutes later Drake was rushing back to the truck to edit the interview and send it to the station. I lingered a moment, unsure of what to say to Eric. Had I only imagined what had passed between us earlier?

"Hold on a sec," Eric said, then disappeared into another room. A minute later he was back, holding a small box. He handed it to me. "This is the gift I was talking about." His smile didn't give me any hint as to what it was. I lifted the lid and couldn't believe what I saw inside.

Swimming goggles.

Don't get me wrong—they were smart-looking eyewear. Electric blue with charcoal eyecups. But they were still swimming goggles.

"I was thinking about what happened to you in Mexico and how you didn't really learn to swim. I want to teach you," he said.

"You what?"

"Instead of running around Lake Hollywood Reservoir, why don't you come twice a week with me to the swimming pool where I train?"

I shook my head. "Yeah, I don't think that's something I'm ready to do right now."

A hot-looking guy like him certainly didn't have to offer to teach swimming to get a date. So what was in it for him?

He grinned. "I'll make it fun. You'll see." He stopped speaking and looked at me as though he were seeing me for the very first time. Then he reached out his hand to touch my hair, his touch almost unbearable in its tenderness. "It'll be fun. Promise."

He leaned in until his lips were a fraction of an inch from mine then touched his mouth to mine in the gentlest caress. His lips surprised me, soft and pliant when the rest of him was sturdy and strong. And his kiss was unhurried, patient. I closed my eyes and willed this moment to go on forever.

His lips dropped to mine again, more demanding this time, sending a shock wave rocketing through my body. Gone was the dreamy intimacy of our first kiss, and in its place was a newfound urgency.

Heat burst through me at the speed of light. I placed my hand on his chest and felt the muscles contract underneath it, and then I knew I was in too deep. Far too deep. Every cell in my body was aching for me to let it run its natural course, let it play out. From the way Eric's body arched against mine, the heat of his hands on my neck, I knew he was heading the same way, too.

The walkie-talkie on his belt squawked a sequence of tones. "Duty calls," he said, reluctantly breaking the kiss. "We can pick this up tomorrow morning—when you go swimming with me."

I shook my head. "Tomorrow is too soon."

"Chickening out already?"

"I need time to get used to the idea of voluntarily submerging myself in water."

"Tomorrow morning," he said, brushing one last lazy kiss across my lips. "Promise we'll go swimming."

In that moment I would've promised almost anything.

CHAPTER SEVEN

Eric moved in water like most of us wished we moved on land. Smooth, graceful, seemingly effortless. His strong arms sliced through the water with rhythmic precision, in perfect synchrony with his legs and torso, so it appeared as if he only had to stroke the water a few times to get across the pool. It looked completely natural for him, as though swimming had been bred into his genes.

I stood at the shallow end of the Olympic-size pool, my stomach shaking as if someone had dropped a jackhammer inside. I might have looked good in the stylish sapphire swimsuit I'd bought on a whim but never worn, but none of that would matter when Eric saw me flailing around in the water.

I hoped he wasn't going to do the whole macho-guy thing and try to convince me how "easy" it was going to be to learn to swim. On the other hand, I didn't want to be coddled like I was a fragile china doll that might break at the sight of the deep end.

As I watched him glide through the water toward me, I considered leaving. I ticked off a list of excuses I could make. "I'm coming down with the flu" might work. "I've got an important assignment at work" was certainly true. But before I had a chance to put one of them to use, Eric had reached my end of the pool.

"You made it," he said, catching his breath.

In one smooth move, he hoisted himself out of the pool and stood next to me.

Wow. I'm glad I didn't say it out loud, but I know it registered on my face. Know how some guys look terrific when wearing certain clothes? Eric looked fantastic wearing only a pair of black swim trunks. Given his line of work, I knew he was in great shape, but I had not expected the muscled arms and the washboard abs. I struggled to keep my breathing steady.

He wiped the water from his eyes. "Hey," he said, seemingly unaware of the effect he was having on me. "Ready to get in?" Honestly, I wasn't sure how I was going to focus on learning how to swim when he looked like that. "Sure," I said, affecting a breezy tone.

"Meet you at the five-foot marker."

He jumped back in the water, leaving me standing there. At first I wasn't sure why he wasn't waiting for me to get into the water, and then I realized he probably figured I'd be less nervous if I could control how and when I got in.

I stepped down the ladder into the water, momentarily shocked by its coolness. On the third rung, I stopped. This was my first time in any large body of water since the accident. The water was only at the level of my belly button, but panic rose in my throat. My legs felt wobbly and weak, and my fingertips tingled. I closed my eyes to regain my focus, but all I could see was the endless ocean swelling above me.

Water is water. It may be part of the ocean and filled with salt, or it may be filtered and shocked with chlorine in a swimming pool. Even so, all water is the same, and I knew it was still waiting for a chance to grab me again, to finish what it started. Was I crazy for giving it a second chance?

I couldn't stand there indefinitely, even though I wanted to, so in one jerky motion, I lowered myself into the water. Even in the shallow end, I was covered up to my shoulders. I curled my toes, gripping the bottom of the pool, and slowly moved about, adjusting to the water's resistance.

Eric swam over to me. "I know you don't *like* being in the water," he said. "But you do look good in it."

"Not as good as you." There, I said it. Casual, of course. Like I was just being friendly. But the thoughts that were going through my head and the feelings that were stirring inside me as I stood just a few feet away, alone in the pool with him, were anything but casual.

"Let's stay here a minute and bounce."

"*Bounce.* Really?"

He nodded. "I want you to see that the water wants to hold you up—that's its nature. No matter what, the water has no problem lifting you."

"Or drowning me."

"Not going to happen on my watch. If I can pull a boy out of thirty-mile-an-hour white water in the pouring rain, I think I can pull you out of an empty swimming pool."

He had a point.

At first I felt ridiculous bobbing in and out of the water like a kid on a pogo stick. But then Eric started bouncing too and splashing a little water at me with a silly grin on his face. And when I splashed back, I forgot how stupid I must have looked.

"When you're ready," he said, "get in a little deeper."

I crept a little closer to the deep end and felt the pool slope beneath my feet. The water was higher against my body, so when I bounced it rose to the V of my neck. I felt wobbly, certain my feet would lose their grip on the slope and I'd slide helplessly into the water's clutches.

Eric reached out and took my hands, and I was no longer aware of the depth but of how close our bodies were in the water, how little we both were wearing, how warm his hands felt.

"When you're in the water, move as it moves. Allow yourself to be shaped by it."

I couldn't imagine allowing myself to be shaped by the water—not without it choking the life out of me. But the way he was looking at me, I knew I had to try.

"Let's try and float on your back." His hand was on the small of my back as I slowly leaned back into the water. I braced for the inevitable moment when the water would pull me under. I was brazenly provoking it, tempting it to try to claim me again.

But as I floated on the water, instead of fear I felt oddly calm. Eric released his hand from my back and allowed me to float a little on my own. I relaxed into the water, inviting it to cradle me. And it did.

I stayed there for probably only thirty seconds, but it seemed longer. Eric was grinning, deeply now, and looking at me as though I were swimming the English Channel. "In a week you'll be doing laps," he predicted.

"Doubt that."

He swam farther into the deep end and pulled me with him. For an instant I glided through the water, pulled by his strong arms. Then his big hands were on my waist, pulling me to him, until our bodies touched, then met. He wrapped one arm around my waist, holding me tightly to him, while he treaded water with the other.

Every cell of my body was tuned to him—the warmth of his skin through my swimsuit, the feel of his body gently swaying with mine in the water, and the possibilities if either of us moved our bodies a fraction of an inch. He pressed his lips to mine in a kiss that sent a ray of warmth through me.

In that moment the surface of the water looked different. Weaker perhaps. Less able to stake its claim on me again. Less.

~⊙

By the time I got to work at five minutes before nine, I was exhausted. I wanted to go home, curl up under my down comforter, and sleep the rest of the day away. I yawned my way back to my desk and was surprised to find Josh waiting for me, his feet propped up on it. Josh and the cameramen rarely hung around the reporters' desks, so I knew something was up.

"Your phone not working? I've been texting you for the last twenty minutes."

I grabbed my phone from my purse and realized I hadn't even glanced at it all morning. Instead of scanning my e-mails and the day's headlines, like I usually did on my way into the newsroom, I had found myself reliving the morning with Eric. Being in the water with him was far more intimate than I ever imagined. But underneath the strong attraction developing between us, Eric was genuinely determined to help me get comfortable in the water. Maybe it was because the water was where he felt at ease and at home. Or, maybe the water was a place where he tested himself, where he confronted enormous challenges and conquered them. Yet I had the sense there was even more to it than that. Something I didn't yet understand.

Josh handed me a cup of coffee. Black. "You're going to need it," he said. "Read this." He handed me a manila envelope addressed to me in care of the station. It already had been opened. "Rob in the mailroom opened it by accident and when he saw what it was and you weren't here, he gave it to me."

I glanced up at him, perplexed by his serious mood, and unfolded the letter inside. Typewritten on cream-colored, expensive-looking stationery, it read:

> *Dear Kate,*
> *I've watched fakes come forward claiming to be me, and*
> *I've seen experts inaccurately speculate about my motives.*
> *Now I want to set the record straight about who I am*
> *and why I've been giving away so much money. I'll send*
> *you instructions on where and when we can meet. Alone.*
> *Good Sam*

He grinned. "Awesome, right?"

I wasn't sure. As much as I was eager to meet Good Sam and interview him, it made me more than a little nervous that he might be just as eager to meet me.

"It gets better. Keeping reading," Josh urged.

> *P.S. To prove that this isn't a hoax and that I'm Good Sam, talk to John Baylor at 88 N. Nottingham. I just put $100,000 on his porch. Go get an exclusive interview.*

"We can get there in fifteen minutes. Tops," Josh said.

I put the letter down. "Susan Andrews is on Good Sam exclusively now."

"Since when does that stop you from getting a story? Especially an exclusive one?"

Josh was right, of course. In journalism school we had been taught that stealing another reporter's story was akin to cheating on a test. But this wasn't stealing Susan Andrews's work or retelling her scoop. It was just following a lead—one that was directed to me—and beating her to it. But was the lead real? "For all we know, this is a hoax, a wild-goose chase."

"Right. And the best way to find out is to check out John Baylor. If he got some money, this letter must be from the real Good Sam. And if it is, he's going to arrange to meet you for an interview, and you—not Susan—will be the one to find out who he is."

I let out a shaky breath. Had the psychic, Melanie Richards, been right? Would I really be the one to discover Good Sam's identity?

~ூ

John Baylor was in complete shock when Josh and I arrived at his house, a cute white cottage in El Segundo a few blocks from the beach and two blocks south of Los Angeles International Airport.

"I didn't tell anyone we received money," he said. "I only got it about two hours ago. I'm still reeling from it all. How could y'all possibly know about it?"

I dodged his question and said we'd received an anonymous tip. Oddly, he seemed satisfied with that answer.

"I went out the front door to run some errands and that's when I saw the canvas bag," he said, beaming. "I wasn't sure what it was at first. But then I saw that lopsided number eight on the bag and I knew. I knew Good Sam had answered our request."

Unlike many of the others who had received money from Good Sam, John Baylor was eager to talk. In fact he was so effusive that I half wondered if he was megadosing Prozac or secretly acting as Good Sam's public relations agent.

He let us record an interview with him in his living room, which had a working wood-burning stove in the corner. You don't see one of those very often in Southern California, and if you do, they're usually for decoration. But John and his wife had worked through all the red tape and EPA regulations so that they could eliminate their heat bill.

He placed the canvas bag, still bulging with cash, on the couch next to him during the interview.

"One hundred thousand dollars can change your life," he said. He was African American, about fifty-five with salt-and-pepper hair and vintage tortoiseshell glasses you usually see on East Coast professors and West Coast hipsters.

"Why do you think Good Sam chose you?" I asked.

"My daughter put up a note on one of the kiosks they have all around the city. You know, the ones where people put up signs, notes, cards, and such to tell Good Sam what they want. My wife has cancer, and Jane thought Good Sam could help."

"Does she understand that Good Sam only gives money away? That he can't cure cancer?"

He considered the question for a moment. "She's six, so I don't think she understands everything yet. All she knows is that the people Good Sam has helped are always smiling and look happy on TV. In her mind Good Sam is as good as Santa Claus."

"How do you plan to spend the money?"

"There's a new treatment available for my wife's cancer, but it's still experimental and not covered by insurance," he said, his voice ragged. "We're going to use Good Sam's money to see if we can beat this thing once and for all."

I served up a softball question next. "If you could say one thing to Good Sam, what would it be?" I asked.

He paused for a moment, and I leaned forward, waiting for an answer. I didn't invent the softball question, so I can't take credit for its popularity in TV news. A good softball question can get you another thirty seconds or so of airtime and pushes the story closer to the coveted top of the newscast. And it also can be good for your career. Look at the experts, Katie Couric and Matt Lauer.

John Baylor pressed his hands together. "I'd say . . . 'Thank you from the bottom of my heart . . . for helping me and my family, Good Sam.' And I'd say, 'If you ever decide to run for public office, I'll vote for you. Because, Good Sam, you understand people.'"

Good Sam had chosen well.

CHAPTER EIGHT

The way my Good Sam story about John Baylor turned out, with sound bites straight out of a reporter's dream notebook, I expected at least a nod of appreciation from David. I knew better than to expect anything more than a grumbled "Good work" or even "Not bad." What I didn't expect was for him to summon me to a meeting in Bonnie Ungar's office.

In the two months since she joined the station, Bonnie hadn't met with any of the nonexecutives, except during last month's Christmas party, when she had come around to every employee, placed a perfectly manicured hand on each shoulder, and expressed her appreciation for "all the great work." So I knew this meeting meant I was in deep trouble. I actually felt a dip in the temperature as I stepped into her mahogany-paneled office.

"Come on in, Kate," she said, her voice as sweet as maple syrup. Bonnie was well into her fifties with no-nonsense shoulder-length brown hair and a slight gap between her front teeth. She was dressed in a black tweed jacket and pencil skirt, complete with Ferragamo pumps in lipstick red.

David and Susan sat in stiff wing chairs facing Bonnie's desk. Susan stared straight ahead, her arms crossed tightly across her chest. David managed a smile, but it quickly faded the instant I sat in the chair next to him.

"I'll make this brief," Bonnie said, her tone turning tight and formal. "We appreciate all your good work on the Good Sam story, Kate. And your interview with John Baylor was a real coup for this news department." She closed a notebook on her desk. "But we've made a decision to position Susan as the lead reporter for this story. David has discussed this with you already. True?"

"Yes."

She leaned back in her chair and clasped her hands together. "Then why have you continued to pursue this story?"

Because that's what a good reporter does, I wanted to say but didn't. "Because Good Sam sent me a letter."

"Good Sam sent you a letter," Susan said, rolling her eyes just enough for me to see the disdain but not enough to look unprofessional.

"Why would he single *you* out?" Bonnie asked.

I shrugged. "I assume it's because I broke the story and my reports have been all over our newscasts for days . . . up until now."

I looked to David for support. "That's true, Kate," he said, his olive skin unusually pale. "Regardless, I made it clear two days ago that we were assigning the Good Sam beat to Susan. Didn't I?"

I nodded.

Bonnie stared at me for a moment, then picked up a pencil and twirled it between her fingers. "Okay, then," she said coolly. "Let's be absolutely clear about what has to happen next. Susan is exclusively on the Good Sam assignment. If you get any further correspondence from Good Sam or any leads related to the story, bring them to Susan and she will follow through on them."

"Why?"

"Why?" she answered, as though I'd just asked her why the earth rotates on its axis. "Because Susan is an established brand with our viewers. They've come to expect her to handle the big stories. And we want to further that expectation and improve our ratings."

"Haven't I improved the station's ratings with my reports on—"

"There'll be no further discussion about this," Bonnie interrupted. "We appreciate all your good work and want to see you continue that work covering the police-blotter stories, but your assignments are not your decision." She dropped the pencil on her desk. "Do we have an understanding?"

I felt Susan's eyes upon me and sensed she was already gloating over her victory. I tried hard not to show any emotion, not even a hint of the anger that raced through my veins.

I glanced at David again, to see if he might rally to support me, but he was reading something on his phone.

"Yes, of course." I said it as though it was a relief to be free of the Good Sam story. I almost believed it myself.

My friend Sarah has a voodoo doll. Whenever someone at work does something that aggravates her, she pushes a pin into the doll's body to instigate a headache, back pain, or a bout of nausea in that person. She works at one of the movie studios in town, so—what can I say?—she uses that voodoo doll a lot.

I wanted a voodoo doll after I left Bonnie's office. Childish, I know, but I had never encountered such an impenetrable brick wall before. I once had a news director who threw things and shouted obscenities when he was angry about a story, but I actually would have preferred that behavior to Bonnie's stone-faced coldheartedness.

As I made my way back to the newsroom, Alex rushed up to me and handed me an envelope. "This just came," he whispered. "Do you think it's from Good Sam?"

The envelope was addressed to me in a showy word processor font usually found in wedding invitations. Typed in red ink beneath my name, the message read:

To Be Opened Only by Kate Bradley. Personal and Confidential.

I had no doubt it was from Good Sam. But after meeting with Bonnie, I didn't want Alex to get into trouble for helping me with the assignment.

"Don't think so. I actually think it's a wedding invitation."

I could tell he didn't believe me. "Are you sure, because—"

"Positive. Thanks, Alex. I'll catch up with you later."

I ducked into an editing bay and ripped open the envelope. The letter read:

Dear Kate,

Now that you've confirmed I'm Good Sam, meet me tomorrow night at eight outside the City National Bank building downtown. Come alone, and don't bring cameras. If I see you're not alone, or if you mention this meeting to anyone, I won't show up.

Good Sam

∽

Downtown Los Angeles at night. Alone. Last year sixteen thousand people were assaulted in Los Angeles. Nearly five hundred were murdered. Most of the crimes didn't happen in downtown Los Angeles, of course, but fear isn't easily swayed by logic.

None of this made sense. If Good Sam wanted the attention, as I suspected, why did he want me to come alone, without a cameraman?

I could only conclude that he wanted me on his territory. On his terms. But why?

A chill ran down my spine, and then I kicked myself for being such a chicken. This was Good Sam—the man who had given away one million dollars.

When I first started on the Bummer Beat, reporting on all the arsons, murders, and robberies, I'd return to my apartment at night so on edge that I'd search for potential killers in the closets and under the bed. I actually walked around with my cell phone clutched in my hand with 911 already punched in.

When David had assigned me to do a live report on three homicides that had happened within a three-hour period in Watts, I'd turned it down. I'd been too afraid to go there at night. Turned out the story got enormous national attention and launched the career of a little-known reporter at Channel Four named Diane Stinson. Six months later she was hosting *Good Morning America* for ABC.

Was I going to let fear stop me from getting my big break? And what about Bonnie's mandate to hand any leads off to Susan?

Maybe David had been right. Maybe I'd have been better off covering the political beat. Although politics can get dirty and scandalous, a reporter rarely has to meet a source alone at night in a gritty part of town.

When I returned to the newsroom, I was surprised to see Eric sitting on the edge of my desk.

"They said I could wait for you here," he said, rising.

My lips softened into a smile. "They won't even let my father sit at my desk when I'm not here. How'd you convince them to let you in?"

"I guess I look trustworthy or something."

"My guess is it's the 'or something' that got you in. If Shondra's at the security desk, she'll let in just about any guy with a cute smile."

"You think I have a cute smile?"

"Cute is for chipmunks. Your smile is . . . tempting," I said.

He took a step closer and touched his hand lightly to my hair. "Could I tempt you into having dinner with me then?"

I glanced at the clock—8:47. "Unless we're going to McDonald's, we'll never get a reservation or a table this time of night."

"Where I want to take you, we don't need a table or a reservation."

"Where exactly do you have in mind?"

"Griffith Observatory. A blanket, a bottle of wine, and hot chili straight from the kitchen of the winners of the Los Angeles Chili Cook-Off."

"Tempting." I glanced at my thin wool pants and matching jacket. "But I'd be freezing dressed like this."

"I'll keep you plenty warm," he promised.

As I picked up my purse from the desk, the letter from Good Sam fluttered to the floor. Eric reached down and picked it up and saw what it was.

"Another fake Good Sam?" he asked.

"Actually, I think this one might be the real deal. He wants to meet me tomorrow night."

"What makes you think he's not yet another fake?"

I shook my head. "Earlier today he gave me a lead about one of the people he gave a hundred thousand dollars to. The lead panned out."

Eric scanned the letter and frowned. "Anyone who asks a reporter to meet him alone downtown at night and demands that she keep the meeting a secret is up to no good. You shouldn't go."

"The Good Sam story is so hot right now that an interview with him would be, well, probably the most important interview of my career."

He fell silent for a moment. "Kate, he could be dangerous. At the very least, someone should go and watch out for you."

I pointed at the letter. "He says I have to come alone."

"How about if I go down there before you, sit around and read the *Wall Street Journal* on my iPad, and act like I'm a suit on my dinner break?"

"As much as I'm curious to see what you look like in a suit, I'll be fine," I said, smiling. "Really. What could possibly happen?"

"He could very easily whisk you away in a car."

"There'll be no whisking," I said, trying to lighten the mood. "Besides, I don't think that's Good Sam's style. I mean, someone who gives away a million dollars probably doesn't have a criminal bone in his body."

He thought about that for a moment. "Someone who gives away that kind of money would either keep quiet about it or meet you on your territory to talk about it," he said softly. "He wouldn't demand that you come alone to downtown Los Angeles at night."

I looked at him, ready to tell him about the dozens of tougher assignments I'd handled on my own. But then I saw something in his eyes I hadn't expected.

Genuine concern. For me.

It was an unfamiliar feeling to be the object of someone's worry, and I wasn't entirely sure I liked it. Did it make me weaker, somehow less capable, if I needed his help?

Eric handed the letter back to me. "I'll be there. He'll never know I'm there. You won't even know I'm there."

I'd been to the Griffith Observatory several times during the day. I'd stood on its balconies, which afforded spectacular views of the city from high atop Mount Hollywood, and even sat through—or should I say slept through—one of the planetarium shows. There's something about lying in a high-backed chair in the dark and listening to a scholar's quiet voice telling you about the stars and constellations that induces immediate relaxation and, for me anyway, sleep.

On Monday nights, the observatory and museum are closed, and after sunset, the trails that lead through the park and up the mountain are also closed. But Eric knew about a fire road, a narrow, twisting back road used by park and fire officials to get to the top of the mountain. As we traveled up the road with only the light of his headlights to guide us, my stomach tightened at every curve.

"You okay?" he asked.

"Fine." I lied. I wasn't just afraid of driving off the mountain. I was afraid of the feelings that were developing inside.

It's like riding a roller coaster. The moment the car crests at the top of the hill, you are completely at the coaster's mercy. You have to trust that the car won't fall off the track and that your seat harness won't break. You have to trust that the other person won't break your heart. I guess that's why I don't like roller coasters; I'm not good at trust.

"We're almost there," he said. "It'll be worth it—you'll see."

Griffith Observatory is a whole other world at night. It's dark enough that you can see the silver stars glittering in the sky above and the golden lights of the city glowing below. And while you know you're in the middle of one of the world's largest cities, it feels as though you've escaped to a secluded sanctuary high above the noise and cars and people.

It was also cool—probably only in the low fifties, but with the kind of mountain dampness that anyone who's been in Los Angeles for very long considers cold.

Eric laid a blanket on the ground and gave me one to wrap around my chilled body. He pointed up at the stars. "It's really clear tonight after the rain. Clear enough that you can see Orion's dagger."

I guess I shouldn't have slept through the planetarium shows, because I had no idea where Orion was. "Orion?"

"See those four bright stars there?" He leaned his head back and pointed to a spot right above us. "The top two are his arms; the bottom two are his legs. The three stars in the middle are his belt, and his dagger hangs below."

You know how some people see scorpions and tigers and women holding scales in the stars? I never could see anything but a jumble of white dots. But that night I could actually make out the pattern.

"I see Orion," I said in amazement.

Eric pointed back up at the stars. "See those bright stars over there? You can see parts of Andromeda and Perseus."

"Where?"

"They're not easy to see, like Orion. I've never seen the entire constellation of Perseus, but I look for the pattern at the top where Perseus is holding the severed head of the Gorgon, Medusa."

I couldn't see Perseus, or Medusa's severed head, for that matter. But I could see the excitement in Eric's eyes as he scanned the skies. He seemed completely at ease underneath the stars—the same relaxed way he'd had in the pool.

"I think I've forgotten all the Greek myths. Was Perseus the Greek Titan who was chained to a rock?"

"You're thinking of Prometheus," he said. "But Perseus's story does have someone chained to a rock. Andromeda's mother, Queen Cassiopeia, told the sea nymphs that Andromeda was more beautiful than they were. So the jealous nymphs got revenge on the queen by arranging to have Andromeda chained to a rock by the sea. The sea rose up to drown Andromeda, and with it came Cetus, the sea monster, to devour her. But Perseus, fresh from killing Medusa, had been watching over Andromeda and fallen in love with her. Perseus flew down, single-handedly slayed Cetus, and rescued Andromeda."

After watching Eric rescue the boy in Malibu Canyon, I could see why he liked this story. Like Perseus, he had flown down to slay the sea monster and rescue the boy from the water.

I relaxed onto the blanket and took in the depth of the skies, realizing I was staring into the past and wondering how many other stories lay out there among the stars. Under their canopy, the day's worries about Good Sam, Bonnie Ungar, and Susan Andrews felt trivial.

"How do you know so much about Greek mythology and the constellations?" I asked.

He lit two candles in mason jars, which cast a warm, yellow glow in the darkness around us. "When my brother and I were little, my father taught us how to navigate a boat by the stars using an old-fashioned sextant. The easiest way for me to remember the constellations is through the stories."

"What kind of dad teaches his kids to navigate using the stars?"

"A dad who loves sailing. We used to take the boat out every weekend when it wasn't raining, and in the summer we sailed almost every day. I spent so much time on the boat or in the water that they used to call me Fish."

"Fish, huh?" I said. "Can you still navigate a boat by the stars?"

"Somewhat," he said. "I cheat and use the GPS a little, but once you learn to do it, you never really forget."

"So you still go sailing a lot?"

"Not anymore."

Something in Eric's heavy tone made me look at him, but he had turned his head away, and I couldn't see his expression.

"Why not?"

He was silent for a moment, and when the words finally came out, they sounded strained. "I just don't."

Call it a reporter's habit, but I couldn't leave it at that. I watched him open and close his hand reflexively and wondered what he was thinking. "C'mon. You're the only person I know who can navigate a sailboat by the stars. Why don't you sail anymore?"

He opened his mouth as if to reply, then quickly closed it. "Can you drop it?"

He stood abruptly and headed to the car, leaving me alone. As I watched him pull some items from his trunk, my cheeks grew hot. Had I asked too many questions? Was I an annoying *pochemuchka*?

Long minutes later he returned carrying a soft-sided cooler. "Hey," he said, and then sat on the blanket next to me. He rubbed the back of his neck. "Sorry about the way I handled that." He twisted the cooler's long straps into a soft knot. "My brother and I used to sail together a lot, and ever since he died, I really haven't been too interested in going sailing."

His words came out sure and steady like they always did, but underneath the calm I sensed there was something more that he wasn't saying. I realized then that no matter how charming and attractive he was, there was something about him that was just out of reach. My instinct was to press the conversation further, to say some words of sympathy about his brother's passing or to coax an answer out of him about how his brother died. But in the flickering light, his eyes seemed to be imploring me not to dig deeper. Not to ask any more questions.

"I know it sounds like a cliché that firefighters make the best chili, but the guys at the station really do," he said, his tone lightening. "They've won the LA Chili Cook-Off two years running. This is their latest experiment."

He pulled two piping-hot cardboard containers from the cooler. Steam rose up and swirled around the containers, infusing the air with fragrant oregano, onion, and a surprising hint of cinnamon. He made a show of presenting me with the warm container and a plastic spoon.

I dug into the chunky chili, which had a major kick to it and an unexpected sweetness. When I looked up, I found Eric stealing a glance at me. I had the definite feeling he wanted to say something, so I waited for him to speak, but he grew silent again.

"This morning you teach me to swim," I said, filling the silence. "Tonight you serve me the best chili ever. How are we ever going to top a day like this?"

He took my hand and held it. "I'm pretty sure we'll find a way."

I became aware, then, of the crisp night air, the slow song the crickets were singing nearby, and the scent of freshly mowed grass. In that perfect moment, all my senses were suddenly and joyfully awakened, and I felt connected to Eric in a way I'd never felt with anyone before.

A slight breeze caressed my cheek. I leaned my head against his shoulder, dizzy and giddy with anticipation. And that's when I knew I was falling. I'd crested at the peak of the roller coaster and was plunging down the other side, trusting him with my heart.

A full moon was high in the sky, lighting our way as we drove back down the mountain. The constellations Eric had shown me—Orion, Perseus, and Andromeda—were now mere specks of light, faded by the moon's bright beams.

Eric's cell phone beeped. He pulled over to the side of the road and read the text. "Damn," he said, slamming his fist against the steering wheel. "Damn."

"What happened?"

"The boy in Malibu Canyon I rescued. He just died."

"No." I closed my eyes, shuttering the tears that threatened to spill out. The water had claimed another victim. It had grabbed and held him in the darkness long enough that not even Eric and his crew's brave maneuvers could save his life.

The last time I'd cried for a victim of a story I had covered was on Good Friday last year. I had gone to the home of a budding high school athlete who had been gunned down the night before while sitting on the front steps of a friend's house. While I interviewed the dead boy's cousin, I felt a sudden rush of heat and thought I was going to vomit. In the middle of the interview, I got up and rushed out of the room. I couldn't come back. Every time I stood up, the room spun and my body broke out in prickly sweat.

I was certain I had an ulcer, or worse, a brain tumor or inoperable stomach cancer. No matter how much antacid I chugged, I couldn't make my stomach stop hurting. After a battery of tests, a doctor told me there was nothing wrong with me—except I spent too much time reporting on tragedy.

Neither Eric nor I spoke for a long time. With only the light coming from the dashboard, I could make out his profile but not his expression. I was sure I saw his body tremble slightly.

"When I went to rescue the boy," he said, his voice snagging in his throat, "I met up with his father, who had accidentally let go of him when they were trying to cross the river together. He said to me, 'My baby's gone.' And the look in his eyes, the way he said it . . . I'll never forget."

I placed a hand on his arm, unsure of what to say. Every tragedy chips away at optimism. Hope becomes fragile then frayed—until one day, if you let it, hope disappears entirely.

"I thought I had a shot at saving him," he said.

"A tragedy like this is hard. But it does get better," I said quietly. "Tomorrow will be better."

He turned to me, the beginnings of a smile on his face. "I wish I had some of your optimism."

"No one's ever called me an optimist before."

I kissed him then. I knew it wouldn't change what he was feeling. But it was a start.

CHAPTER NINE

Anyone who tells you downtown Los Angeles is dead hasn't been there in a while. At eight o'clock, City National Plaza, a large patch of concrete between the two City National Towers, is filled with people going to dinner or on their way home. The plaza is part of what they call the "new downtown," known for its gleaming sky-scrapers of steel and glass, home to the Pacific Stock Exchange and the financial district. It's probably the one area of LA where you won't see many tourists toting cameras, because it looks like just about any downtown anywhere.

I sat on a metal bench beneath the glare of fluorescent park lights and waited. In the distance I saw the 444 Flower Building, now the Citigroup Center, also known as the *L.A. Law* building because it appeared in the opening credits of the show. That program has been off the air for over two decades, but the label still persists. From the ground, the building doesn't look glamorous the way it did in the aerial TV shots. If this building were in Manhattan, no one would even notice it.

I couldn't see Eric anywhere. I wondered whether he'd realized he'd overreacted about the danger involved and decided not to come after all. It certainly didn't feel dangerous with so many people mill-ing around and the traffic noise behind me. I scanned the crowd, knowing any one of these people could be Good Sam. Was it the dark-haired man in the Brooks Brothers suit holding a cell phone to one ear and pressing his finger into the other? Or could it be the man with the Kindle tucked under his arm who was glancing at his watch?

There were so many questions I wanted to ask him. "Why did you give so much money away?" "Why did you stamp the number eight on all the bags?" "Why did you keep your identity a secret?" "How did you choose the people you were going to help?" "Why did you choose *me* to tell your story?"

Where was he? Too much time was passing. Was he watching me right now, making sure I'd come alone? A shiver ran up my spine, but I resisted the urge to shake it away.

"Kate, is that you?" I heard a man's voice say.

I turned to my right and squinted into the streetlight to see a tall man walking toward me with two other men. I felt my blood go ice cold.

It was Jack.

"It is you," he said. "What are you doing down here?"

I swallowed hard; I thought maybe I would choke. "I'm meeting someone."

Jack had changed his look in the six months since we'd broken up. His wavy hair was cut short, and he was dressed more formally than I remembered, wearing a Versace sport coat with a pair of dark slacks.

"I never would've expected to see you here." He turned to the two men. "This is Kate Bradley, my former fiancée," he said. "Kate, these are two of my clients from New York, Bob and Shaun."

I stood. Bob and Shaun extended their hands to shake mine, but even as I did so, I felt Jack's eyes bearing down on me.

"Kate's a reporter for Channel Eleven," Jack said. "Maybe you'll see her on the news while you're in town."

"I'm an NPR guy myself," Bob said. "Don't usually watch the local news. Too many murders and shootings."

"It's an acquired taste," I said smoothly, but I was a jittery mess. I felt Jack looking at me. If a look could bore a hole, I was pretty sure he could see straight through me to the *L.A. Law* building.

"We're late for our meeting at Capital Group, Jack," Shaun said, glancing at his watch. "We'll call you tomorrow to give you those numbers. Nice to meet you, Kate."

"You too," I said, but the words caught in my throat.

I watched the two men head off in the direction of the Bank of America building.

"Please, can we sit for a moment?" Jack asked.

I sat down and Jack joined me on the bench, but I followed the departing men with my eyes, not wanting to look at him.

"God, it's good to see you," he said, resting his arm on the back of the bench. "Mind if I keep you company while you wait?"

I did mind. I was sure Good Sam wouldn't approach me if he saw Jack sitting next to me. No doubt he would misread the situation and assume I hadn't followed his instruction to come alone.

"I'd rather you didn't, Jack," I said. "I'm meeting someone any minute and—"

"Who're you meeting?"

I crossed my arms. "I can't explain right now. But I really need you to leave."

"I've missed you," he said, ignoring my plea. His sincere tone made me look at him for the first time. I regretted it instantly because Jack had a quality about him that turned my brain to mush. Maybe it was his eyes, blue like Texas denim, with a hint of mischief in them. Whatever it was, it was wreaking havoc on the rational part of my brain.

"I didn't mean to sound so harsh," I said. Why was I apologizing?

"You look great," he said softly. "Even more beautiful than I remember."

I stood. "We'll have to catch up another time. I really need to go."

He leaned forward and spoke so softly I almost couldn't hear him. "Are you here to meet Good Sam?"

I straightened. "Why do you say that?"

"Because I'm him." Or at least that's what I thought he said. But there was so much noise around us that I must have misheard.

"What did you say?"

"I'm Good Sam." He broke into a smile and waited for his words to sink in.

"And I'm Diane Sawyer," I said. "The truth is, I'm meeting Good Sam, and I need you to leave because he said to come alone or—"

"I wouldn't show," he said quietly.

I felt the blood drain from my face. "The letters from Good Sam—*you* wrote them?"

He nodded. "I can prove I'm Good Sam."

My voice sounded reedy and thin. "Why? Why did you do it?"

"I made a lot of money on a recent IPO, and I figured that rather than spend it on more expensive clothes or a faster car, I should give some of it away. But I didn't want to give it to a foundation and let someone else choose where it should go, so I decided to practice, you know, random acts of kindness."

"Random acts of kindness." I didn't hide the sarcasm in my voice.

"Or whatever you want to call it."

His face began to swim before my eyes. I waited for the dizziness to pass before I spoke. "But why like this? Why all the secrecy? Why didn't you just call me and tell me?"

"The way things were between us, I was pretty sure you wouldn't believe me. I knew you'd want proof. So I gave you the proof you needed."

He touched his hand to mine and looked me in the eyes. I was more confused than ever. My bullshit radar told me he was selling me a line, in the smooth, casual way he used so successfully with his clients. I reminded myself that this was a man whose bible was *The Greatest Salesman in the World*, by Og Mandino. But there was a part of me that wanted to believe him—that *did* believe him.

"Why don't we go to the station and record this interview in the studio?" I suggested.

Jack shook his head, and his expression darkened. "I won't do an interview. I don't want the media attention. I'm in way over my head here, Kate, and I was hoping you'd help me figure out what to do."

A lead block formed in my chest. *He wasn't going to let me interview him.*

He cleared his throat. "I'll tell you everything . . . but not here. Let's go somewhere quiet. I have a car waiting for me on Flower."

He stood up and held out his hand to me. I searched his face for some hint that he was playing with me, but all I saw was his wide good ol' boy smile.

"Okay," I said, but I didn't take his hand. "Let's find a quiet restaurant where we can talk."

"I have a suite at the Biltmore. Would you join me there?"

I stopped and looked at him. I knew firsthand how a casual dinner with him could transform into something else after a few glasses of wine and some quiet talk on the couch.

"Don't worry," he said, as though reading my mind. "As much as I'd like to, I'm not going to try to seduce you back into my life."

As we started across the plaza, he placed his hand on the small of my back. It was the gesture of a lover, too cozy for my comfort. But I didn't ask him to stop; I was still clinging to the possibility of an interview.

A black limousine was waiting for us in a loading zone on Flower Street. Jack slid into the backseat and instructed the driver to go to the

Biltmore. I was about to slide in next to him when I felt a strong hand on my arm. I glanced over my shoulder.

It was Eric.

"Everything all right?" he asked.

"Yes, fine," I said, wishing I could telegraph to him not to worry. But even then I'm not sure he would have believed me. I had promised him I wouldn't get into a car with Good Sam, and here I was doing exactly that.

"You need help?" He clamped his hand tighter.

"I'm okay."

"Hey, take your hand off her." Jack jumped out of the car and tried to pry Eric's hand off my arm. But Eric was a full head taller and much stronger. His hand didn't budge.

"Stop, Jack," I said. "I know him."

Jack let go of Eric's arm, and his eyes settled hard on mine. "I told you to come alone."

I considered saying it was a coincidence running into Eric downtown but decided Jack needed to hear the truth. "We thought it was risky for me to come down here alone. Eric came to keep an eye on me."

"Well, you've done your job, Eric," Jack said. "She's in good hands."

Eric looked at Jack, then back at me. "Are you sure you want to do this?"

"Yes, Jack and I know each other."

"I'm her fiancé," Jack said, wrapping his arm around my waist.

I shot him a withering look. "You're not my fiancé."

"You still have the ring, don't you?" Jack said with a wicked twinkle in his eye.

The color drained from Eric's face. "You're not Good Sam?"

A taxi behind us honked.

"We're blocking traffic. Good to meet you, Eric," Jack drawled, then slid into the limo and pulled me with him.

"I'll call you later," I said to Eric, my eyes pleading with him for understanding.

As the car drove away, I watched Eric standing on the sidewalk, an expression of sheer confusion on his face.

I felt exactly the same way.

When Jack said he had a suite at the Biltmore, for some crazy reason I imagined a master bedroom with a separate sitting area. I should've known better. This suite, aptly named "The Biltmore," had two bedrooms, a full gourmet kitchen and pantry, a dining room with a conference table, and a living room the size of my entire apartment. Its deft mix of sleek contemporary furnishings with mahogany and cherry antiques created a style that could only be interpreted as power.

Jack always had entertained in places like this. Even though his own style was more southern traditional, he knew his clients liked doing business in a setting that exuded the appearance and style of old money. For his wealthiest clients, it was a world to which they were accustomed. For the others it was the world they aspired to—a place of luxury they, too, could inhabit if they invested wisely with Hansen Investments.

I wondered whether he had brought me here to sell me something, too. Had he lured me here pretending to be Good Sam while the real one was still out there?

He shed his suit jacket, which looked as if it had been tailor-made for his tall, trim body, and carefully laid it across the back of a chair. "What can I get you to drink?"

"Nothing." I heard my voice tremble a little. How could he be so calm?

"Are you sure? Because I can have them bring up a bottle of wine. Or maybe champagne? We ought to have something to celebrate getting back together."

"We're not back together."

He grinned. "We're here. And we're together. Aren't we?"

I didn't argue. "Nothing for me. Thanks."

Jack poured himself a gin and tonic and sunk down into the buttery leather couch. "You're still surprised it's me, aren't you?" he said. "And you're not sure I'm telling the truth. Am I right?"

I nodded, pretty sure my voice would shake if I spoke.

"I always could read your mind." He rested his head against the back of the couch. "That's what made us so great together. You could read me like a book, too."

"I can't read you right now." My voice was surprisingly low. "If you are Good Sam—"

"And I am." He motioned to the seat next to him. "Sit. If I know you, you've got a thousand questions. Tell me what's on your mind."

I knew he expected me to sit on the couch next to him, but I chose the club chair instead. I pulled my cell phone out of my purse. "Let me call the news desk and have them send over a cameraman."

"That's not what this is about. I don't want the media attention. I don't want anyone to know I'm Good Sam. Promise me you won't tell anyone."

I shifted in my seat, feeling like a bird whose wings had been clipped. I swallowed hard. "Okay."

He turned toward me. "Now, what do you want to know?"

It struck me as odd that he seemed so comfortable, so casual about what he'd done. Didn't he realize the sensation his actions had caused?

"How did you do it? Did you drive around dropping off sacks of money at random?"

He rubbed his left shoulder. "I hired a guy to do the physical act of dropping the money on the front porches. I didn't want to run the risk of being seen, especially once the media started swarming."

"What's the significance of the number eight on all the bags?" I asked.

"Maybe you should be shining a light in my eyes, because your tone makes this feel like an interrogation."

"I have a lot of questions."

"I know, but you're so serious. This is *me* you're talking to, Kate . . . you know, the guy you promised to marry. Your fiancé."

I opened my mouth to say something, then I shut it. I wasn't going to be bitter, so I softened my tone. "You are not my fiancé."

"I was once. For twenty-seven days. What did you do with the ring?"

"I still have it." The ring was too expensive to throw away, even though I wanted to. I'd considered sending it back to him but decided it wasn't safe to send a two-carat diamond ring even by FedEx.

"Then there's still hope," he said softly.

I looked away, refusing to meet his gaze. "Again, what's the significance of the number eight on all the bags?"

"You don't remember?"

I shook my head.

He sat up. "You really don't?"

I shrugged. "What am I supposed to remember?"

"Vegas." He reached across and touched my leg. "Your lucky number."

It all came back to me then. My first trip to Las Vegas, my first time playing the craps tables anywhere. Our first weekend trip away together.

"Every time you played the number eight, you won."

"We ended up with something like four thousand dollars before the night was over." I smiled, remembering the thrill of effortlessly winning so much money.

"And remember the casino sent over those two beefy security guards to keep an eye on us like we were running some kind of scam? They kept changing out the dice because they thought we had a phony dice thing going on."

"I don't think they believed us when we told them eight was just our lucky number that night," I said, then sobered. "So that's why you put the number eight on the money bags?"

He nodded. "It was a lucky number for me, too." His voice was warm and low. "That was the night I realized I was falling in love with you." His words hung in the air and swirled around me, drawing me to him. I looked into his blue eyes and remembered falling in love with him, too—the way he looked at me as though he'd never seen anyone more beautiful, entire weekends where we didn't get out of bed until late afternoon. I remembered feasting on Texas barbecue and ridiculously priced champagne, late-night skinny dipping in his pool, and riding up the Pacific Coast Highway together with the top down and the stereo at full volume.

"I messed up, Kate. I really did. Nobody's perfect—certainly not me. And cheating on you was the biggest mistake of my life." He leaned forward, caressed my hand. "You have to know that it would never happen again. If we got back together—"

My plans to avoid sounding bitter went out the window. "When I saw you kissing Ashley in the elevator that night, I had believed you when you said it was a one-time thing and that she initiated it. Do you have any idea how humiliating it was to find out that you actually were sleeping with her all along?"

Then my mind took one of those wrong turns it often did, and I imagined Jack with Ashley. As hard as I tried to shut it out, I couldn't erase the image or the sick feeling in the pit of my stomach.

"I'd hoped we could move past all that," he said quietly.

I felt my body vibrate with anger. "I found out the truth about you and Ashley at our engagement party. How am I supposed to move past that?"

"I told you it was a mistake . . . a big, stupid mistake."

"I trusted you," I said through clenched teeth.

"I've said I'm sorry. I've sent flowers and cards. Tell me, Kate, how else can I make it up to you?"

I sat there silently, my heart racing. All the feelings came back to me. Anger. Humiliation. A deep ache that had dulled but never fully gone away. "Let me interview you," I said impulsively. "On camera."

"Is that what it's going to take?" He stood. "That's all you want from me?"

"An exclusive interview. You can't be interviewed by anyone else. Only me."

He drained the last of his drink. "Fair enough," he said. "It's not what I want, but if it means so much to you, I'll do it."

It felt too easy. There had to be a catch. And there was.

"But after the interview, you'll have to let me take you to dinner." He leaned forward. "Don't say no just yet. If you still hate me after the interview, you can say no. Otherwise you have to say yes."

Why did he have to be so charming when I wanted so much to dislike him? I reminded myself that I was here to get an interview, not fall under his spell again.

"Okay. Can we shoot the interview tonight? I can have a camera crew down here in thirty minutes."

He glanced at his watch and grimaced. "Can't. I've got a late dinner meeting. Let's do it first thing tomorrow morning when we'll all be fresher. I'll come to the station."

I stood. I needed to get out of there before things got intense between us again. "I'll need the proof before tomorrow morning, Jack. Copies of statements showing the withdrawals—"

"I know what you need. I'll have my assistant e-mail everything to you tonight."

"Exclusive, remember? You can't talk to anyone else."

"Exclusive."

Before I knew it, he leaned forward, cupped my face in his hands, and kissed me. I can't say that I didn't like it, because I did. It reminded me of the taste of him, of the excitement of being with him for the first time, of another time. Before.

I broke off the kiss. His eyes searched mine, trying to gauge my reaction. "That guy, Eric. He isn't—"

"He isn't anyone we're going to talk about." I headed for the door. "See you tomorrow. Ten o'clock sharp."

❧

David Dyal wasn't rubbing his ear. He was pounding the desk with his fist.

"What did we agree on in Bonnie's office yesterday?" he shouted. "Weren't you supposed to hand off any leads to Susan?"

My temper flared, but I kept my voice calm. "He contacted me and said he wouldn't show if I brought—"

"You should have given this to Susan."

"I score the interview that every network and news outlet has been vying for, and all you can say is that I should've given this to Susan?"

He stared at me and then slowly sank into his chair. "How do you know he's the real deal?"

"Jack and his father own Hansen Investments, one of the largest investment banking firms in Southern California. We sent the proof Jack provided to Phil Hayden, the forensic accountant we used on the bank-scam story last month. He reviewed the records and confirmed that Jack did earn north of a million dollars on an IPO a few weeks ago. He also confirmed that Jack withdrew over a million dollars from various accounts in the last few weeks."

"That doesn't mean he actually withdrew it to give it away."

"Right. It only proves that Jack has the means to give away that kind of money. But you should know that his father is William Hansen."

"Treasury secretary under Carter?"

"Reagan."

"That gives him credibility," he said. "But why does a guy like that give so much money away like this?"

"He says he did it because he wanted to give directly and anonymously. He never expected all the media attention."

"You expect me to believe that a guy like him—a guy who grew up in a political family whose every move was followed by reporters—didn't expect a media frenzy when he anonymously gave away a boatload of cash?"

"Did any of us expect this kind of reaction to this story?" I asked quietly. "Who would've thought viewers would be obsessed with the Good Sam story when the biggest stories last week were the train collision, the freeway chase in Gardena, and the bank shoot-out in Burbank?"

David tapped a pen on his desk. "Let's say for the moment he's the real deal. Why did he pick you to tell his story?"

I sucked in a deep breath. "I knew Jack before he came forward as Good Sam. We were engaged once."

He stared at me in complete silence. "That isn't reassuring me," he said finally. "In fact that's a real problem. Your objectivity is compromised."

"No other reporter will be tougher on him than I will be."

He sat in his chair and rubbed his temples. "Viewers won't see it that way. They'll see that you're not an objective news reporter but a biased former fiancée." He took a swig of his Dr Pepper. "Why didn't you marry him?"

"A lot of reasons. Reasons that are between him and me."

"Your private life will become part of the story. You want that?"

"Not really. No."

"You've got to see there's a serious conflict of interest here." He was silent for a long moment, tapping his pencil on the desk. "Susan should do the interview. Viewers will perceive her as more objective."

Although I knew he was right, I felt like I'd been socked in the gut. "He won't do the interview with anyone but me," I said, enjoying the power in those words. "He gave me an exclusive."

"We'll see about that," David said.

CHAPTER TEN

There'd be no network debut for me. No local prime-time special. No exclusive interview. No report.

Good Sam, Jack, didn't show. It was past eleven—more than an hour past the time we'd set for the interview—and David had assembled the station's best crew in studio one. Our top director, Theresa Myers, had been pulled off another assignment to direct this segment, and the set had been lit with the careful attention usually reserved for distinguished guests like the governor or George Clooney.

Some of the staff had gathered at closed-circuit monitors around the station to witness their first glimpse of Good Sam. But all they saw were two empty chairs on the interview set.

I'd chosen to wear a red sweater dress with a long gold chain, one of the most camera-friendly dresses in my wardrobe. I'd even arrived more than an hour early so that the hair stylist could blow-dry my hair to perfection. All for nothing.

"What do you mean you can't find him?" David demanded. His face was bright red, as though he were suffering from a bad case of windburn.

"He's staying at the Biltmore, but they say he's not in his room," I said.

"We also paged him at the hotel," Alex added. "But he's not anywhere on the grounds."

"I called his office at Hansen Investments, and they tried his cell, but he didn't answer," I said. "His secretary said he sometimes forgets his phone and carries another phone. But she couldn't give out that number."

David downed the rest of his Dr Pepper. "I've got every executive at this station and two people at the network waiting for this interview. What are you going to do?"

I felt sweat break out on my upper lip. Was it better to end the humiliation now and cancel the interview? I wasn't sure I could stand any more frustrated looks and doubtful glances from the crew as they waited impatiently for Jack to show.

"Maybe Good Sam's decided to give his exclusive interview somewhere else," Susan offered to no one in particular.

I didn't even have to look at her to know she was enjoying this awkward moment.

"I'll give him ten more minutes," David said. "Then we shut this baby down."

That's when I remembered the cell phone Jack had sent me for my birthday. Hadn't he said he'd programmed all his phone numbers into it? I ran back to my desk, grabbed the cell phone from my top drawer, and pressed the "On" button, praying the battery hadn't run down.

The ping of the phone turning on was the sweetest sound I'd heard all morning. I scrolled through the preprogrammed numbers. Sure enough, Jack had programmed in all his numbers: "Jack—Home," "Jack—Work," "Jack—Cell," and "Jack—Cell2." I pressed the button for "Cell2" and waited for it to ring.

"Hello," he answered.

"Jack, where are you?" I said with steel in my voice.

"On my way to see you."

"You said we'd do the interview at ten. We've been waiting for over an hour. What's been keeping you?"

"Sounds like you've been missing me," he said, his tone silky smooth. "Have you?"

What was he talking about? "When we didn't hear from you, we thought maybe you weren't coming."

"Now why would you think that? I'd never walk out on you like you walked out on me."

His words hit me full force. Was he being deliberately late just to make a point? To make me pay for walking out on him at our engagement party?

I bit my tongue. "When do you think you'll be here?"

"You sound like you missed me. I like that."

"When will you be here, Jack?"

"About fifteen minutes. I guess the cell phone I gave you came in handy after all. Didn't I say you'd want to use it to get hold of me?"

As he hung up, my stomach clenched in a knot. I was beginning to worry about the price I'd have to pay for this interview with Good Sam.

Like a rock star who had kept his fans waiting, Jack Hansen strode into the room projecting nothing but radiant self-confidence. Dressed in a tailored dark blue suit, white shirt, and crimson tie, he was the perfect image of a successful businessman, definitely the kind of person who one might imagine could be Good Sam.

Every eye in the studio was on him as he took my hand in his and pressed a kiss to my cheek. "Sorry I'm late."

David stepped forward and extended his hand. "I'm David Dyal, Channel Eleven's assignment editor."

"Good to meet you, David," Jack answered.

David wasted no time in making his case. "Look, Jack. There's a serious conflict of interest here because of your relationship with Kate, and we'd prefer that you did the interview with another one of our award-winning reporters, Susan Andrews." He motioned toward Susan, who was standing by a teleprompter, fully made-up and ready to do the interview.

Jack glanced at her and then laid his gaze on me. "I understand your predicament, David. I do. But if that's your decision, then I won't be doing an interview with Channel Eleven."

David rubbed his ear. "Understand that being interviewed by Susan is not only best for Channel Eleven, but given the circumstances, it's also in your best interests."

"I'll decide what's in my best interests," Jack drawled. "And now it seems it's not in my best interests to do an interview at all." He turned to me. "I'm sorry, Kate. I think you know I didn't want the media attention. And I only agreed to go on camera because you were going to do the interview."

As he headed toward the door, my stomach sunk to the floor. But that was nothing compared to what Susan Andrews must have felt, because the look on her face was complete, utter shock. In her entire career, I'm certain no one had ever turned down an interview with her. Not with her classic beauty and gentle, West Texas lilt.

"Wait." David called after Jack. "Let's see if we can work this out."

With the frantic energy that comes from waiting around for two hours, the sound guy clipped a microphone to Jack's lapel and hid the wire in his jacket. As the lighting guys scurried around making minor adjustments now that Jack was sitting in the chair, David waved me over to a corner of the studio.

"Bonnie's giving you the green light to do this interview," he said. "But only if you get Jack to sign an agreement granting the network an exclusive. For seven days he can't be interviewed by anyone else."

I flipped through the eight-page document in a type size only a fly could read. "You want me to get him to sign this right now? On set. Before the interview."

He sighed. "All right, do the interview first. But when it's over, get him to sign it. Once this story airs, he's going to get calls from just about every reporter and journalist in the country. We need this to be exclusive."

I took my seat on the set across from Jack. I didn't like needing anything from him, yet I was beginning to feel my entire career depended on what he did in the next several minutes.

"Guys," Jack said, addressing the crew, "I'm very sorry for being late. I know you all have busy schedules, and I appreciate your waiting for me."

That got bonus points with the director, Theresa. "I'll wait for you," she said my earpiece. "How come you're getting to interview all the good-looking ones lately, Kate?"

I was still too nervous to even crack a smile. My pulse raced so fast that I was sure the microphone clipped to my jacket could pick up the sound of my thudding heartbeat. It wasn't only the crushing pressure of doing a good interview, but after my phone conversation with Jack, I worried there'd be a stiff undercurrent to it as well.

I needn't have worried. Jack was one of the smoothest, most dynamic people I'd ever interviewed. Considering that most of the interviews I'd done before had been with the victims of—and witnesses to—crimes and disasters, that wasn't saying much, I know. But Jack eased into the interview as if he were born to be on television.

"For the past two weeks, much of the country has been speculating about the identity of the man who anonymously gave away one million dollars to Los Angeles residents. Thousands of inches of newsprint and countless minutes of airtime have been devoted to this person, a man we've been calling Good Sam," I said. "Yesterday, Jack Hansen, cofounder of Hansen Investments, admitted he was behind the generous and anonymous gifts. Jack, are you Good Sam?"

"Yes, I am," he answered.

"Tell us why you gave away so much money."

"My investment firm has done extraordinarily well. When a recent investment did better than I'd expected, I decided to give away all the profits, which totaled well over a million dollars. There's no point in earning money if you can't use it to make a difference."

"How did you decide who would receive the money?"

"Most charities already target the poorest people in our communities: the homeless, the chronically unemployed, the unskilled, those living well below the poverty line. I think that's important and necessary. My philosophy as Good Sam is this. It's not only those who've hit rock bottom who deserve help. Corporate mergers, globalization, recessions, tax cuts for the superwealthy—these all have the effect of punishing all Americans. What about those who appear to be getting by on their own? The man who works two jobs to put a roof over his family's head, who pays his taxes, yet still fights to make ends meet? He doesn't qualify for food stamps or low-cost housing or handouts from charities. He's laboring longer, earning less, and has fewer job protections than he did twenty-five years ago. Yet few government programs or charities address his needs."

"Yet some of the people you helped were not needy or poor. For example, you gave to a professor and a neurosurgeon. Why?"

"You're right. I gave to people in a wide variety of professions and financial circumstances. But most of the money went to the people who keep the factories and stores running, who fix our cars and our plumbing, who bake our bread and serve our coffee, who teach our children in school. They are the soldiers of our everyday lives, and they cannot and should not be forgotten."

I'd never heard Jack speak like this before. He was eloquent, sure of himself, and solid in his convictions. "Why did you give the money anonymously?"

"The best way to give is when neither the recipient nor the donor knows the other's identity. I never wanted or expected the attention this simple act of giving would attract."

"Then why come forward now?"

"Many people were claiming to be me, and my actions were being appropriated and twisted by others for their own purposes. I wanted to set the record straight about who I am and what I'm hoping to accomplish."

"Will you continue to give as Good Sam?" I asked.

"Absolutely." He cracked a smile. "Although it appears that it'll be difficult to continue to give anonymously."

David's voice came though my earpiece. "Ask him the significance of the number eight on the bags."

I hesitated, knowing Jack's answer could subject me to questions about our relationship. "A lot of viewers are curious to know why you stamped the number eight on the canvas bags that held the money."

He met my gaze and held it. "Let's just say that eight is a lucky number for me. I'm not the superstitious type, but that number has brought me and those I love good luck a number of times."

"What's your reaction to all the attention that's being paid to Good Sam?"

"I have to say I'm not all that comfortable with it. I don't think such a big deal should be made about giving away money—something all of us in higher-income brackets should be doing anyway. But I'm starting to see that it's an opportunity to get people thinking about their own giving and how they, too, can make a difference."

"Your father is former treasury secretary William Hansen. What does he think about what you've done?"

"Well, actually, I haven't talked to him about it, but I think he'd approve. He always says the greatest thing you can do is to help others."

I knew when the interview was over that it was the best interview of my career. As much as I was proud of myself for handling it, I was even more amazed at Jack. His answers were polished and short—perfect for television. And he exuded a kind of charisma I'd seen only in powerful executives and high-ranking politicians.

"Great interview," Theresa said, shaking his hand. "You're exactly how I hoped and imagined Good Sam would be."

"Thank you." He met her gaze. "I appreciate your waiting for me."

I found it curious that many of the crew waited to meet him—I'd rarely seen them attempt to talk with any of the dozens of guests and celebrities who shuttled through the studio every year.

David came out of the control booth with the beginnings of a smile on his face. I knew I'd done well even if he wasn't going to tell me.

"Just got off the phone with the network," he said. "The nightly news wants a segment for the six thirty cast and a package for an *Evening Edition* newsmagazine special at eight."

I'd never had a story air on the network in front of eight million viewers before. Certainly never had one on a prime-time newsmagazine. So I should be forgiven for the dizzy grin on my face and the giggle that sprang from my throat even as I wanted to appear calm and composed about it.

"But remember . . . ," he went on. Notice how there was always a "but" in David's sentences? "Get Jack to sign that agreement."

I watched as Jack spoke to each crew member, listening to each of them as though whatever they were saying really interested him. This wasn't the Jack I knew. This Jack had a self-confident quality that made you feel you were in the presence of someone important.

Although I tried to resist, I found myself getting caught up in the flush of being around him again, too. I tried to analyze what it was that was slowly drawing me back to him like a moth to a flame. Then I realized I was falling for Jack because he was Good Sam.

He was everything I imagined and hoped Good Sam would be. At the same time, he was what I didn't think existed—someone doing good without ulterior motives.

"Was it everything you wanted?" he asked when the crew had filed out.

I smiled. "Couldn't have been better."

"Then I'm glad," he said softly. "I'm happy we're together again, Kate."

I looked away, uncomfortable under his soft gaze.

"We make a great team," he said.

I handed him the agreement. "Look, I need you to sign this agreement saying your interview is exclusive to this network for the next seven days."

He riffled through the pages. "Pretty tall order, don't you think?"

"It's just giving me what you already promised."

He grinned. "Must be important to you, then."

I nodded, not wanting to acknowledge just how important it was.

"If I'm going to do you a favor, you'll have to do one for me." He took my hand in his. "Have dinner with me tonight. You don't have to, of course, if you still hate me."

That was the problem. I didn't hate him right then. I felt admiration and curiosity, a mixture of the familiar and the wholly new.

"I don't hate you," I said quietly.

"I'll send a car to pick you up at seven thirty." He flashed me his trademark southern-boy smile. "Normally I'd have my attorneys review this before I sign it, but I'm trusting you."

He pulled a pen from inside his jacket and dashed off his signature. "Starting tonight I hope you'll start trusting me, too."

We finished editing the package for the network at 2:28, two minutes before the deadline to load it on the satellite uplink. It was entirely my fault that we'd cut it so close. The network had committed ninety seconds to the story in the evening news, which meant we had to take a Cuisinart to the interview and chop it down to its very core. The result was a package that felt like a here's-a-lot-of-stuff piece to me, filled with facts but very little context. To the utter chagrin of the producing and editing team, I pressed to redo it. The final package was better, but how much story can you tell in ninety seconds?

When it aired on the network at six o'clock eastern time—three o'clock in Los Angeles—a few of the newsroom staff gathered around one of the monitors and applauded. It was a heady experience, one I'll never forget, but there was little time to celebrate because we still had to produce a special that would air in a few hours. After we'd wrestled with the ninety-second segment, it should have felt luxurious to have twelve minutes to tell the story, but even that didn't feel like enough. Time is funny that way.

The network and Channel Eleven exploited the special in every way possible. Not only were they promoting it seemingly every other minute on the air, but the network also had bought ads all over the Internet touting the interview.

"He gave away one million dollars in a few days' time." The announcer's voice boomed in the commercials. "Tonight TBC brings you an exclusive interview with Good Sam. Find out who he is and the surprising reason he's giving away so much money. Exclusively on TBC."

"It's got Emmy written all over it," Josh said when he saw the final product.

Humility aside, I had to agree that it was my best work to date. But although I could take credit for the writing and reporting aspects, it was the story itself that made it great television. How many news stories do we see about someone anonymously and generously helping others? Truth was, we're more likely to see stories about husbands murdering their wives, politicians suspected of killing their interns, and children being abducted than stories about generosity and good.

"Ratings will go through the roof," Josh predicted.

I floated on a cloud all the way to the town car Jack had sent for me. But as I got into the car, something was gnawing at me. I had the definite feeling I'd forgotten something, but I couldn't put my finger on it. With a pang of guilt, I realized I'd never called Eric. If he'd switched on the TV or gone online at all, he already knew I hadn't been mugged by Good Sam and I'd gotten the interview I wanted. Still, he'd gone out of his way to watch out for me, and I'd repaid him by ignoring him.

I pulled my cell phone from my purse and started to dial his number, then ended the call. He was sure to ask about Jack's claim to be my fiancé, and I wasn't ready to explain all of it, especially when I didn't understand it myself.

The next thing I knew, the car stopped in front of Toscana, a quiet restaurant in the heart of Beverly Hills. It's not a place where news reporters like me eat often, because the tariff is steep for even the simplest cuisine. A bowl of tomato soup is fifteen dollars. A cheese plate is twenty-one.

It looked busy. Something like thirty people were gathered on the sidewalk outside the door, waiting for tables. Jack always knew how to pick the new, hot places to eat.

As soon as I stepped out of the car, I knew something was wrong. Like a swarm of bees, everyone on the sidewalk headed in my direction. Some flashes went off, blinding me momentarily. *Paparazzi.* I froze. Had they mistaken me for Jennifer Lawrence or some other celebrity? I could only hope.

A petite redhead shoved a microphone in front of my face. "What can you tell us about Good Sam?"

Then everyone started talking at once, and the space between them and me became narrower and narrower as many of them pushed to get in closer.

"What is your relationship with Good Sam?" someone shouted. "Is it true Jack Hansen is running for governor?"

The flashes were coming so frequently and from so many different angles that I felt like I was under a manic strobe light.

I didn't know what to do. Even if I had answers to their questions, I was pretty sure I couldn't have put together a coherent sentence. I also was beginning to worry about my physical safety as the circle crushed in around me. I've always had a touch of claustrophobia, and my anxiety mounted as I realized there wasn't a clear escape route.

I should have felt a kinship with the reporters who besieged me. I know how hard they have to work to get a story. But theirs was an alien world to me. Even the most chaotic crime scene paled in comparison to the jostling and maneuvering occurring on these ten square feet of sidewalk.

I took a step toward the door to see what they'd do. Even as they continued to shout questions at me, they moved along in step with me.

Then the redhead stepped in front of me, barring my way to the door. "One of the talk-radio shows is claiming that Jack Hansen was your husband. Is this true?"

I found my tongue. "Jack Hansen and I were never married."

I should have kept my mouth shut, because my response sent the crowd of reporters into an immediate uproar, slinging questions at me, only louder.

A strong hand gripped my arm. I pulled away, angry that someone had the audacity to grab me. Then I saw it was Jack pulling me from behind the circle of reporters. He stepped toward me and headed into the crowd, cutting a swathe through the swarm of reporters, straight to the door of the restaurant.

"That's Jack Hansen," someone shouted. The flashes started going off again. The restaurant door flung open, and the second we stepped inside, it was swiftly closed, shutting the noise outside.

Every eye in the restaurant turned to look at us.

"This was a bad idea. When I made the reservation, I never imagined we would cause such a scene," Jack said, then guided me through the restaurant into the kitchen and out the back door, where his limo was waiting for us. We barely had gotten in when the driver gunned the motor and sped down the narrow alley.

Jack touched his hand to my face and angled it toward him. Before I knew it, he was kissing me. This wasn't the exploring kiss of a new lover but the demanding kiss of a lover who already knew what he wanted. So many emotions ricocheted through me that I couldn't sort them out. Relief from the paparazzi. Surprise. Familiarity. Excitement.

His kiss deepened and became more urgent as his hands roamed the length of my torso, grazing my breasts.

"I can't do this," I said, breaking the kiss and pulling away.

He looked like I'd slapped him. "What do you mean?"

"I can't go through with this. Not the way you want me to."

He leaned back in his seat, ran his fingers over his lips. "Did I misread something, Kate? Because I could've sworn during the interview, and afterward, too, that there was a spark between us. Like before."

"Maybe it wasn't such a good idea to go to dinner together." I didn't want to admit that I'd been giving him mixed signals.

"You owe me this."

"I owe you?"

He swallowed hard. "You talk about me cheating on you. But how about what you did to me? You walked out on me, left me to tell our friends and family—at our engagement party—that we weren't getting married. Do you have any idea what that felt like?"

I could imagine how embarrassed he had felt. And when I walked out on him ten minutes into our engagement party, I reveled in doing to him what he'd done to me. Sometimes anger has a way of short-circuiting one's brain.

Now, looking at him, I felt a deep remorse for the first time. They say revenge is sweet, but if that's true, it's only temporary. At some point you must realize that your revenge has made you no less culpable than the person who did you wrong in the first place.

"You owe me another chance," he said, "not only for deserting me in front of our friends like that but also for what I did for you today."

"What you did for *me* today?"

"Our interview will catapult you to the top of the news business. Where you belong. You'll be able to exploit this to get whatever you want."

I crossed my arms. "No one forced you to do the interview."

"No, but I stood up for you, Kate. When your boss tried to make me do the interview with another reporter, I refused to do it with anyone but you. That's got to count for something."

I couldn't argue, because for once what he said was true.

"That's why I did it, you know . . . to help you," he said softly.

My eyes narrowed. "You admitted to being Good Sam to help me?"

"In a way," he said. "It's one of the reasons I gave away the money, too."

"What're you saying?"

"I have to admit it was in the back of my mind while I was giving it away—that someday I'd tell you about it and you'd see I'm not such a bad guy after all. And it worked. You came looking for *me*. I liked that."

"Let me get this straight. You're saying that you gave away a million dollars to strangers just so you could get my attention?"

He combed his fingers through his hair. "You're taking it all too literally, Kate. But I think a part of me was hoping to get your attention, yes."

A question can be as lethal as a weapon. It can insinuate, humiliate, aggravate, and, yes, illuminate. That's why I continued to question him so sharply. "So all that stuff about giving anonymously . . . that was just posturing?"

He shook his head and straightened. "Of course not." He raked his fingers through his freshly clipped hair. "Why are you doing this? Why do we end up fighting when all I want is to get back together?"

I looked down at my hands. An awkward silence fell between us. I wanted to get out of the car and escape the tension, but what would that accomplish? At the same time, I couldn't continue like this, picking at old wounds.

"Let's go back to the hotel and have dinner like we planned," he said quietly. "We won't talk about the past. We'll celebrate the Good Sam interview, and that's all." Then he added, "And if you want, I'll try—really try—not to kiss you again tonight."

Room-service food at the Biltmore is better than what they serve at most full-service restaurants. Jack ordered lavishly, asking them to prepare items that clearly weren't on the regular menu—my favorite dishes, like mango chicken, Thai barbecued beef, and pad woon sen.

We stuck to our promise and talked about everything but our past relationship. He told me about the work he'd been doing as a member of the board of directors of the American Red Cross. We laughed about how his golf game had worsened after he'd followed some advice from Tiger Woods. He asked me how it felt to be on the Bummer Beat and surprised me by naming many of the stories I'd covered in the past month.

"I made a special effort to watch for you on TV when I was in town," he said softly.

By the time I turned to leave at ten, my head was spinning—from the smooth merlot he'd ordered that I'd drunk like water and from spending the evening with him again. Being with Jack was like watching fireworks—surprising, thrilling, commanding my attention, but leaving me ultimately breathless and exhausted.

As I was about to leave, he pressed a single warm kiss to my lips. His mouth lingered close to mine for a long moment, as if he were debating what to do next. In the haze of the moment, I wouldn't have minded if he had continued to kiss me; I would've liked to stay in his arms a while longer. I hated myself for that.

"I'm keeping my promise," he said, then pressed a chaste kiss on my forehead. "You'll see you can trust me again."

CHAPTER ELEVEN

I woke up in a world I hardly recognized. As I flipped the channels on the TV, nearly every talk show was buzzing about my interview with Good Sam. Even though they couldn't interview Jack because of our exclusive arrangement with him, they showed clips from the interview and dissected his philosophy with political and economic pundits. The *LA Times* even weighed in, publishing an editorial on the opinion page titled "What We Can Learn from Good Sam."

By the time I got in to work that morning, I felt completely overwhelmed. My desk looked like a paper plant had exploded around it. Hundreds of people had sent e-mails to Good Sam's attention, and the overnight staff had simply printed them out and placed them all on my desk.

"Last night's exclusive interview with Good Sam," David said in the assignment meeting, "got us the highest ratings in the station's history for that time period." After the cheers and applause died down, he went on. "Thanks to excellent work by Kate, who got us the interview every station in town—and every major network, I should add—wanted."

Everyone turned to look at me, all of them smiling. Everyone except Susan. Her face lacked any expression, and I wondered whether she'd finally made her peace with the Good Sam story.

"Couldn't have done it without Alex," I said.

Alex grinned. Internships at any major television news operation are always fast paced and demanding, but few interns get the chance to work on a story as big as Good Sam.

"We're going to air an encore presentation of the interview again Thursday night," David said. "In the meantime this thing is big. I want team coverage on it. Alex, tell them about the Santa Monica call."

"A businessman in Santa Monica called to say he's started a Good Sam club," Alex said, clearly excited to be participating in the assignment meeting. "The club will follow Jack Hansen's philosophy and give anonymously."

"Has he got any members?" Ted asked.

"He claims he's already got forty members and their first Good Sam deed was to leave four hundred dollars in the mailbox of a young family who badly needed a new set of tires."

"He's probably not the only one starting a club like this," David said. "Susan, find out if there are any other Good Sam clubs sprouting up in Southern California."

Susan nodded her head a fraction of an inch and looked straight at me. I detected a flash of something in her eyes. Was it too much to hope for reconciliation? Then she snapped her eyes back to her notepad.

"Charles, get reactions to Good Sam," David continued. "Interview a waitress, a kindergarten teacher, a hotel maid, a laundry worker, a postman, that kind of thing. Find out what they think about what he's said. Kate, we're going to want you to put together a follow-up story on Good Sam. See if you can get him to talk to some of the people he's helped. Find out their reaction to learning his identity. And get him to tell them why he chose to help them. Guys, this is going to be fantastic television. Highly rated, award-winning television."

When the meeting was over, a few of us stood, eager to dig into our assignments.

"Excuse me," Susan shouted. Everyone turned to look at her and quickly grew quiet. "Are we all going to avoid the elephant in the room.

I mean, are we?" She looked around and scanned the faces of the reporters around her. "If no one else is going to say it, I will," she continued. "Some of the talk-radio shows and tabloids are saying that our Good Sam reporter is Jack Hansen's fiancée. If this is true, it compromises the integrity of this news organization and everyone in this room. So what I want to know is, is it true?"

David answered before I could. "You answered your own question. Look who's reporting it—trashy tabloids and talk-radio shows. Since when do they get the story right?"

"Yeah, well, one of those trashy tabloids—as you call them—printed a photograph of our reporter getting cozy with Jack Hansen in Las Vegas."

I remembered a photograph being taken by a friend of Jack's when we went on our trip to Las Vegas, but the guy was an investment banker, not a tabloid photographer. Had he sold it to them?

My face heated up, and I began to flush. Would everyone else see that as an automatic sign of guilt?

"Your silence isn't answering the question, Kate," Susan said. "I think we all deserve to know."

I looked to David for help—or at least some clue for handling the situation—but he glanced away and rubbed his ear. I was on my own.

"Jack Hansen and I were engaged," I said. A few of the reporters groaned. Charles threw his pencil at the table; and everyone started talking at once.

"But . . ." I raised my voice, trying to be heard over the din. "But that was six months ago. We're no longer involved."

"So your dinner with him last night at a romantic little restaurant in Beverly Hills and later at the Biltmore Hotel was strictly business?" Susan said with complete disdain. "Keith and Brian were talking about *that* on their radio show this morning, too."

"It was strictly business," I said, looking her in the eye as I punctuated each word.

"Right," she said with finely tuned sarcasm. She looked around the room again. "What I'm saying is that it's an odd set of circumstances. The mysterious Good Sam turns out to be the fiancé of the very reporter working on the story. I don't know about anyone else, but I'm having a hard time swallowing that angle."

I tried not to let Susan get to me as I headed to Cristina Gomez's house that morning. As much as I hated to admit it, she had a point. My past relationship with Jack did complicate things. It didn't just make the story problematic; it made me feel conflicted as well.

Now that Jack had helped me, it was clear he expected something from me. He wanted things the way they were before. Before the cheating. Before I walked out.

I couldn't deny that I felt something for him, sparked by admiration for what he had done as Good Sam. It was as though he had changed and the new Jack had become all the things I had wanted him to be: generous, genuine, and truly doing good. Had it simply been the wine, the excitement of the evening? Or was I falling for him all over again?

Jack had agreed to meet me at Cristina Gomez's house so we could tape his meeting with her. When Josh and I pulled in front of her house and I saw the Channel Two news helicopter buzzing overhead and all the TV news vans lining the streets, their antennas rising above the treetops like silver spires, I knew we needed another game plan. If Jack showed up here, he'd be stampeded in a nanosecond. So I called Jack and suggested that we meet on a quiet street a few blocks away.

Ten minutes later Josh and I waited on deserted Hardy Avenue as Vince Gill sang "Next Big Thing" on the radio. Jack's limo pulled up, and thirty seconds later, we were on our way back to Cristina's house.

"Take off your jacket, shirt, and tie," I told Jack.

"What for?" he asked.

"We've got to get you into Cristina's house without you being recognized."

Jack smirked. "So you're hoping I won't attract attention if I go in naked?"

"You're going to look like our cameraman. There's a station polo shirt and hat in the back. You'll carry the camera inside. With any luck no one will notice you."

When we got back to Cristina's house, I began to worry that the plan wouldn't work. At least a dozen reporters had gathered on the sidewalks. Some of them surely would recognize Jack. I glanced back at him, now fully dressed in the guise of a cameraman, and laughed. Even in an oversize polo shirt and a crummy hat, he had a bearing about him that said "wealth" and "power," not "photojournalist."

Josh got out of the van and organized the camera equipment. Then Jack hoisted the equipment onto his shoulder, tilted his hat over his eyes, and headed toward Cristina's front door. I curled my toes, wishing he'd hurry up, but Jack took his time, like a real cameraman would.

Thankfully most of us see only what we expect to see. That seemed true for the reporters and neighbors standing in front of Cristina's house anyway. As Jack walked by loaded down with heavy equipment, no one even glanced at him.

Cristina's official introduction to Good Sam was a made-for-television event. Tears rolled down her cheeks as she thanked him in a mixture of English and Spanish. She told him she desperately needed money after her husband had lost his job and explained how Jack's gift had arrived at just the right time. She detailed how she planned to spend the money and how she planned to be a "*un* Good Sam *pequeño*" herself, a little Good Sam, by anonymously giving away some of the money. Jack was visibly moved by what she said and several times was completely speechless.

"How did you know I needed help?" Cristina asked quietly. "How did you pick me?"

Jack was silent for a moment. "All I can say is that I did a little homework," he said with a twinkle in his eye, which prompted Cristina to give him a big, theatrical hug.

After we wrapped up the interview, Jack's attention shifted. He kept checking his watch and began pacing, periodically glancing out the front window.

"I have a meeting at noon downtown that I can't miss," he said. "I've asked the driver to pull around to pick me up. You finished with me?"

I nodded. It seemed strange to think he was going to conduct any meaningful business with anyone today. Surely none of his clients would want to talk with him about venture capital and tax shelters when the topic on everyone's minds was Good Sam.

The limousine pulled up. In one swift move, Jack opened the front door and pressed a long, hard kiss to my lips; then he dashed to the car. I was caught off guard, surprised that he had the audacity to kiss me in public and mortified that people might have seen us, further compromising this story and my journalism career.

I quickly scanned the crowd to see if anyone noticed. Several of the people on the street turned to watch Jack sprinting to the limo, but none of them seemed to be looking at me. Then Jack's limo sped away, its tires squealing.

That's when I saw Eric.

He was dressed in his dark blue firefighter uniform and talking with Kristin Michaels, a willowy blonde reporter from Channel Two, the top-ranked news station in the market. She didn't have a microphone in his face, so I assumed she wasn't interviewing him. I could also see from the way she smiled and played with the ends of her hair that they weren't having a weighty discussion about, say, the Middle East crisis.

I'd admired Kristin Michaels ever since I came to work in Los Angeles. No TV reporter can cobble together more dramatic footage for a news package than Kristin. She has a kind of charisma and approachability that makes people want to talk to her, and her ease in front of the camera makes her one of the best at ad-libbing a live news report. Still, I didn't like the way she was looking at Eric. Or the way he was smiling back at her.

I crossed the street. As I walked toward them, Eric turned to look at me. Then it hit me how much I'd missed him—and how stupid I'd been not to call him.

"Kate, how are you?" Kristin asked. "We met before at one of the mayor's press conferences. I'm Kristin Michaels."

"Yes, of course. Good to see you again," I said, surprised she remembered me. I turned to Eric. "Hi," I said, but it sounded weak and drippy.

"I see you made it back in one piece," he said quietly.

"You two know each other?" Kristin asked, motioning at Eric and then at me.

"We do," Eric answered.

"Was that Jack Hansen we just saw tearing out of here in a limo?" I nodded.

"I have to say that all of us at Channel Two are more than a little envious of your exclusive interview with him," Kristin said. "How did you manage it?"

"A little luck," I said. Normally I would have used this opportunity to crow a little, since it was usually Channel Two that got the exclusives, not us. But I had no appetite for bragging—not with Eric standing there. "Can I talk with you a moment?" I asked him.

"Sure," he answered flatly, then turned to Kristin. "Thanks for your help."

"No problem," she said with a toothy smile. "Like I said, it's got to be one of the tabloid reporters' cars that's blocking your car. Those guys don't care where they park."

When we had walked far enough away from her, I said, "I'm sorry. I meant to call you after the meeting downtown, but things have been a little crazy these past few days."

"I can see that," he said, with a bitterness that surprised me.

An uncomfortable silence fell between us. The sound of the leaves crunching beneath our footsteps filled the air.

"What brings you here?" I said, trying to find something to say to break the silence.

"We were doing a training session a few blocks from here. I saw all the news helicopters and came to see what was going on."

"Are you still game to give me another swimming lesson? I've been practicing holding my breath in the shower." I tried, in a lame attempt to inject some levity into the conversation.

He stopped and turned toward me, squinting into the sun. He didn't say anything for several beats, which made me even more nervous. "I'd say you've got your hands full with Good Sam, or whatever your fiancé is calling himself."

"Jack and I are not engaged—well, we were once. A long time ago but—"

His tone hardened. "From what I saw a few minutes ago, I'd say you're very much back together."

"Jack, well, he just doesn't . . ." I stopped, irritated at myself for bumbling. It sounded like I was lying. "I'm spending time with him because he's Good Sam."

"Or so he says."

"He's got proof." I didn't elaborate. I figured Eric was envious of the attention Jack was getting, and I didn't want to make it worse by pointing out everything Jack had done.

He glanced at his watch. "Look, I've got to find the person who's blocking my car."

He started to walk toward his car; then he turned around. "Why don't you ask your Good Sam again why he gave money to the Ellis family, who obviously are quite wealthy? Have him explain that."

He walked away without looking back.

A few mojitos with Teri at our neighborhood California-Cuban restaurant, Xiomara, didn't dull the ache much. While the kiss Eric saw Jack plant on me complicated the picture, I couldn't understand why Eric didn't believe me when I told him my relationship with Jack was over.

Then again, maybe Eric knew me better than I knew myself. In quieter moments, I had to admit I was conflicted about my feelings for Jack. I didn't trust him any further than I could throw a nine iron, but how could I *not* feel admiration and awe for his actions as Good Sam? Anyone who felt such conviction about helping working Americans and was willing to back that up by giving generously must be good.

"Eric's jealous," Teri said, as I started on my third mojito. She had her hair twisted in a slightly messy chignon, which made her look even more sophisticated than usual. "You know how guys can be sometimes. Look at it from his perspective—you and Jack are in the news everywhere together. That would make even the most secure guy a little jealous."

"If he were jealous, you'd think he'd want to spend more time with me, not push me away."

"That's where being rational doesn't help you," Teri said. "Because maybe that's how *you'd* react, but it's obviously not what he'd do. What's the Mars and Venus thing again? You know, how men have to go into their caves to process their emotions? Anyway, that's what it is. Jack is a wealthy, attractive guy who's the focus of national attention right now, and Eric thinks he can't compete."

"I think you watch too many daytime talk shows."

"Guilty and proud of it," she said, raising her hand. "Thank God for my DVR, because I couldn't survive modern life without my daily fix of *Dr. Phil* and *Ellen.*"

"If you knew Eric, you'd see he doesn't need to be jealous of Jack."

Teri frowned. "What? Is Eric being talked about throughout the country right now? Did he give away a million dollars anonymously?

Are Good Eric clubs being formed around his philosophy?" She lowered her voice. "I don't see how anyone could compete with that, Kate."

"Eric puts himself at risk every day to save lives. I don't see why he'd feel threatened by Jack's notoriety."

"I don't see why you even care about how Eric feels," Teri said. I looked up, surprised at her callous tone. "Don't kill me for being honest, but have you got two eyes? Why are you even thinking about Eric? What's not to like about Jack Hansen right now?"

I slumped in my chair.

"Hear me out," she said, waving a fork at me. "Let's forget for a moment that Jack is Good Sam with a message that's catching on across the country. We'll just call that icing on the cake, okay? But what's important is that he wants you back. He could have anyone he wants right now. And he wants *you*. And he's doing everything in his power to win you over. Why can't you let him?"

I smoothed a wrinkle in the checkered tablecloth. "Remember when I covered the story about the pregnant wife who disappeared, and I kept telling you I had a feeling the husband knew something about it? I ended up being right about it. It turned out he'd killed her."

"I'm not following you," Teri said, shaking her head. "Are you saying you think Jack is a murderer?"

"No, I'm saying I have an uncomfortable feeling about Jack. He seemed a little strange after the interview with Cristina Gomez today. Like he was supposed to be doing something else. Like he *wanted* to be somewhere else. Something about this afternoon felt . . . off. And my reporter's instinct is usually right about things like that."

She waved at the waiter and then pointed to her empty glass. "Maybe with all the excitement around this story, your instinct is dead wrong. Maybe you've got to tune out all the Good Sam stuff and listen to what Jack's saying to you. Really hear it. And then you'll realize he's still very much in love with you."

"Maybe that's part of the problem. I wonder if Jack is in love with me. Maybe he's only in love with the idea of *having* me. Jack always wants most what he can't have."

Teri sank back into her chair and shook her head. "There you go—overanalyzing this. Why can't you just accept that he's crazy about you?"

"Two summers ago, Jack lost a big golf tournament," I said, draining the last of the mojito. "Turned out the winner was an investment banker too—an *entry-level* investment banker. For months after that loss, Jack practiced day and night, got himself the most expensive coaches, bought better clubs—everything. It totally consumed him. Not because he loved the game of golf but because he thought the other guy had gotten something he should have won. I wonder if that's how Jack feels about me. I'm something he should've been able to get, but I got away."

CHAPTER TWELVE

I don't make it out to Pacific Palisades often. With its sprawling mansions fortressed behind electronic gates and stone walls, few crimes are reported here. It's a city with a median household income that's three times that of the rest of Los Angeles, where the new money of Hollywood celebrities and high-tech instant millionaires coexists with the moneyed establishment.

So when I pulled up to the brooding cliff-side mansion in the Riviera section, the most fashionable part of the Palisades, I definitely felt out of my element. Jack had asked me to meet him there for a dinner party.

I'd said no at first, not wanting to fuel any more rumors about our relationship, but I finally relented when he told me the dinner party was being hosted by Senator Tom Wintour, a man who'd served in Congress with my father for more than a decade. Knowing the party was at the Wintours' gave me a level of comfort because I knew they'd never allow other reporters into their exclusive compound.

A valet opened my door as soon as I stopped the car. I heard the sound of piano music as I stepped through a long tree-lined walkway lit by thousands of twinkly white lights. At the end of the walkway loomed a three-tiered Spanish-style mansion alongside a shimmering waterfall infinity pool and 180-degree ocean and city views.

I was about to knock on the front door when my cell phone chirped twice, indicating I had a text message from Alex. It read:

Rumor that Jack H. is running for US Rep. 33rd District. Confirm?

My heart froze. I read the message again in case my eyes were deceiving me in the dim light.

They weren't. Jack apparently was running for Congress in a district that covered Beverly Hills, Malibu, Pacific Palisades, and Palos Verdes—places where residents had recently received money from Good Sam. *Was Good Sam simply a setup for Jack's congressional campaign?*

I would've discarded this as yet another crazy rumor born during the Good Sam media frenzy (one rumor was going around that Jack was Bill Clinton's secret love child), but Jack had told me many times that he planned to follow his father into politics someday. I had always assumed that day was a long way off. But why would it be?

A slender woman with high cheekbones and a blonde bob answered the door. "Kate," she said warmly and then gave me a brief hug. "Candace Wintour. We met when you were a teenager."

I recognized her name, of course, but couldn't remember seeing her before. Not surprising. When I was growing up, my father frequently socialized with others in the political stratosphere, and their faces and names were always a blur. Almost all the men had thick heads of hair, even those well past sixty, so it was hard to distinguish one from another by their hair. So in my teens, I'd developed a kind of shorthand for remembering them, or at least something about them. "Garlic breath, turkey neck" was a congressman from Nevada. "Basset hound, watery brown eyes, orange suntan" was a senator from Georgia. "Glasses, toupee, close talker" was a congressman from Pennsylvania.

"Nice to see you again," I said, as though I remembered her.

"I understand your father is in DC this week," she continued. "That's unfortunate. We would have loved to see him."

She led me into the living room, where about two dozen others, most of them my father's age, were gathered in small groups. I recognized a few of the faces. A congressman from Northern California. A senator from Arizona.

Not knowing what the tone of the party would be, I'd dressed in the most conservative of the two black dresses I owned. Given all the Chanel and Louis Vuitton on the women in this room, I'd chosen wisely.

I spotted Jack across the room with a group of men dressed nearly identically in dark blue suits, light blue shirts, and colorful ties. When he saw me, he crossed the room, took my hand, and introduced me to the man he'd been speaking to, a burly guy with a healthy head of gray hair and bushy eyebrows shaped like giant commas. "Kate, this is Tom Wintour. He and my father were roommates at Harvard."

"Last time I saw you, Kate, you were in high school," he said. His voice was hoarse, like he spent a good part of his day talking. "Your father and I served a couple of terms together then."

"Yes, of course. Good to see you again, Senator Wintour," I said, remembering him. But as I looked at him, my mind flashed to . . . candy. Chocolate candy with fluffy caramel centers.

"*Former* senator," he said.

I studied his face, and this time my mind flashed to pink and green mints. "Was your desk in the Senate chamber called the candy desk?"

"It was," he said. "I kept it stocked with candies, chocolates, anything sweet."

"I remember that, too," Jack said excitedly. "When I visited as a kid, I always made a beeline for your desk."

"Me too," I said, sharing a laugh with Jack.

"You two and every senator around," Tom said. "The desk got so much attention that the Chocolate Manufacturers Association started sending me free candy."

"The caramel candies with the nougat centers," I said, closing my eyes. "To die for."

"I liked the chocolate mints best," Jack said. "I've tasted a lot of chocolate since then, and nothing compares."

"Well, with any luck, at some point down the road you could be sitting in the candy desk yourself, Jack," Tom said, and patted him on the shoulder. "I'm getting another scotch. Can I get either of you anything?"

"No, thanks," Jack and I said in unison.

After Tom left to refill his drink, Jack turned to me and smiled a broad South Carolina grin. "Darlin'," he said, exaggerating his accent, "you look wonderful tonight."

"Don't," I said quietly.

"Everything okay?"

"I just heard a rumor that you're planning to run for Congress and—"

"Damn," he said; then he lowered his voice. "I wanted you to hear it from me first. Come out on the terrace with me for a second."

I followed Jack out the French doors at the other end of the room and onto a balcony with a panoramic view of Santa Monica Bay. The sound of the ocean was like background music, slightly hushed so as to not drown out the conversation, as though the superrich and powerful could even orchestrate that, too.

"Only a handful of people know it yet, but I've decided to run for Congress," he said. "In the thirty-third district. The current representative, Charles Campbell, is stepping down at the end of his term and my advisers think this is a good time for me to announce my candidacy to succeed him. I know this is a lot to take in but I've bought a house in the district. In Calabasas. You'll love it. It's got plenty of space for—"

"When did you decide this?"

"I think it was decided thirty-six years ago, when I was born," Jack said, without a hint of irony. "It was always a given that I'd get into politics someday. You know that."

"Odd timing, don't you think? Deciding to run for Congress right after all the Good Sam frenzy."

"C'mon, Kate, don't twist this," he said, his drawl thickening. "I've been evaluating opportunities to run for office since I was old enough to vote. After all the Good Sam attention, my advisers thought the timing was right for me to run for an open US representative seat. That's all this is."

"But you're running in the thirty-third district, Jack. That's the same area where you—as Good Sam—gave away most of the money. Are you going to tell me that too is just a coincidence?"

"I swear to you, I didn't decide to run for Congress until *after* I gave the money away."

I thought about his Good Sam TV interview. Had it been too polished? Too carefully crafted? "Your whole thing about helping the people who keep the factories and stores running and who fix our cars and our plumbing—that wasn't about Good Sam. That was your platform statement, wasn't it?"

"I meant every word of it."

I remembered Eric's comment that the Ellis family was wealthy, not middle class. "So how do you explain Michael and Marie Ellis?"

"Who?"

"One of the families to whom you gave a hundred thousand dollars."

"What about them?"

"If you did your homework, you'd know the Ellises are quite wealthy. Michael Ellis is head of neurology at St. Joseph Hospital."

He rubbed his jaw. "I might have made a mistake then."

"It's a pretty big mistake, Jack. Surely you would have researched your targets to make sure you didn't end up giving a hundred grand to a guy who probably makes that every month."

He combed his fingers through his hair again. "If what you say is true, then I screwed up. I'll look into it first thing in the morning."

"It'll be in my next story," I said quietly.

His tone darkened. "Why do you have to report that?"

"That's what I do. I report the truth."

"Don't, Kate. It doesn't serve your purposes to burst this bubble we're both in. You have as much at stake as I do," he said. "Look, would it make a difference if I told you that your father is backing my bid for Congress?"

I felt something snap inside me. Resentment and bitterness short-circuited my brain. I opened my mouth to reply, but words failed me.

"He's going to call you later to tell you himself," he continued.

Jack mistook my silence for disbelief. But for once I believed what he was saying was true. I just couldn't believe that while he was working me on the Good Sam angle, he also had the audacity to be working on a political favor from my father.

Jack had met my dad several times when we were dating. It had surprised me back then how easily their friendship was forged over a shared interest in golf and history, particularly the Civil War. Jack even read some of the history books my dad had recommended. I thought he had befriended my father in order to win me over. How could I have been so naive?

I bit my lip, angry that he thought he knew my weaknesses so well. "I need to get out of here."

"Don't." He took hold of my wrist. "You did that once before to me, and I never got over it. Maybe I deserved it then. But you can't do that to me now. These men and women are going to back my bid for Congress. If you walk out now, you'll make me look like a complete failure."

"So that's what this is about, isn't it? You want me back in your life because you don't want to look like a failure for losing me."

"No, that's not what this is about." He loosened his grip on me. "I love you."

"Do you, Jack? Or do you love Kate Bradley, the daughter of Senator Hale Bradley? The well-connected wife to help you with your political ambitions."

He ran his fingers through his hair. "I do love you. I always have. You have to believe that."

"We've been looking all over for you two," Candace said, swinging open the terrace door. "Dinner is served."

Jack held out his hand to me. I didn't want to cause a scene in front of Candace Wintour. But as I followed Jack back into the living room, I wondered what price I would pay for staying.

The skies cooperated the day Jack announced his intention to run for election in California's thirty-third district. The press conference took place outdoors, in the plaza of a trio of office buildings in Santa Monica, a backdrop that was designed to command attention and give Jack an aura of authority and leadership.

Not that he needed to worry about getting attention. Every media outlet in town had come, covering every square inch of the plaza with reporters and cameras and microphones. Officially all they were told was that Jack Hansen, the man known as Good Sam, was going to make an announcement. Many plugged-in news organizations had heard the rumor that he was running for Congress, and although that kind of news didn't usually warrant live coverage, many stations still opted to cover it live, knowing that anytime a Good Sam story was on the air, ratings soared.

I took my place at the front of the pack, directly in front of the podium where Jack would soon be standing. As I waited for Jack to come out, I realized I was as angry with myself as I was at him. I'd let down my guard, let him suck me into the Good Sam story, never fully realizing he might be manipulating me for his own benefit. Jack had that effect on me. Being with Jack was like standing in the midst of a brilliant sunbeam, dazzled by its radiance even as you knew it was burning you.

That radiance was on display as he made his announcement. Flanked by my father and several other well-known politicians and businessmen, he had the handsome, healthy look of a well-connected candidate on his way to Congress. He had mastered the image—the strong, authoritative hand gestures; the decisive facial expressions, and a solid delivery with the right amount of charm and sincerity.

From the expressions on the faces of the reporters around me, they seemed to be buying the idea that Jack had decided to run for office *after* all the Good Sam attention. After all, this was Good Sam, the man who had anonymously given away a million dollars to complete strangers. He was one of us—a little richer perhaps—but nonetheless someone we could trust.

Dark clouds were beginning to form on the horizon as Jack spoke. A few fat raindrops spattered on us, but then, as so often happens in Los Angeles, the rain stopped. Jack had a lot to say about education, taxes, and poverty—all the usual candidate hot buttons. But it was his closing remarks that would really grab viewers' attention: "We should remember that the concept of the Good Samaritan is not found in the Constitution, which explains why government has been an abysmal failure at reducing the ranks of the poor and needy. But more government isn't the answer. We need to encourage businesses, organizations, and individuals—through tax incentives and other programs—to do their part. So that the people who keep the factories and stores running, who fix our cars and our plumbing, who bake our bread and serve our coffee and teach our children in school have a chance at the American Dream."

But after Jack finished his presentation and reporters were allowed to ask questions, the afternoon took on an almost surreal feeling. Every aspect of it seemed like made-for-television news, manufactured into perfect sound bites with precision planning and exceptional photo opportunities.

I didn't have any actual proof that Jack had created the Good Sam event in order to build awareness for his political campaign. It was only a hunch. Instinct. I had hoped to ask my father what he knew about the timing, but I could never get Jack away from him long enough to have a private conversation.

Back at the station, that uneasy feeling stayed with me as I worked with Alex on editing the interview.

"Okay, what's up?" Alex asked as we sat in the editing bay watching the playback of Jack's press conference for the eighth time.

"Nothing," I said. "I just want to get this edit right."

"I think you've gone through something like a pound of M&M's while we've been in here. What's on your mind?"

"This is what's bothering me." I fast-forwarded the clip to Jack's closing remarks. Alex looked confused. "Seems pretty straightforward to me. Kind of inspiring, actually."

"Jack says he wants to give these people 'a chance at the American Dream' but he didn't seem to know that Michael and Marie Ellis, to whom he gave a hundred thousand dollars, were already quite wealthy. Michael Ellis is head of neurology at St. Joseph Hospital. He was already living the American Dream long before Jack gave him money."

Alex scratched his head. "So maybe he made a mistake and the money was supposed to go to someone else? Is that what you're thinking?"

"To be honest, I don't know what to think. Something about that gift, something about the sequence of events just feels . . . off."

"Follow the money."

I shot him a quizzical look.

"You know, from the movie, *All the President's Men*. Deep Throat tells Bob Woodward that all the answers to his questions can be found if you 'follow the money.'"

"Aren't you a little young to be quoting that movie?" I asked.

"You know that movie is like a journalist's textbook."

I nodded. I'd first seen the film in high school, and it had inspired me to think about a career in journalism. It made a reporter's work—even the constant pressure and the arduous work of tracking down leads—look exciting, even thrilling.

The editing bay door opened, and David's voice startled me from behind. "There you are, Kate. I need you and Josh to head back out right now and cover the storm situation in La Crescenta. Thunderstorms are dumping so much rain there that they're bracing for mudslides in the mountains. Several big homes are in jeopardy and they're evacuating the area."

He sure knew how to pitch a story to get my heart pumping. I grabbed a station-issued storm umbrella and started out of the edit bay; then I stopped and turned to Alex.

"Call Phil Hayden, the forensic accountant who reviewed Jack's financial statements, and ask him to make a list of each cash withdrawal from Jack's account and then match it up to the times that each of the Good Sam recipients got their money," I said. "Let's follow the money."

CHAPTER THIRTEEN

The rain pounded Los Angeles throughout the afternoon. Carl, our morning weatherman, had predicted we'd get slammed with a half inch today. But since Carl spent more time worrying about his receding hairline than analyzing weather patterns, I was pretty sure he was wrong. The way the rain was falling in sheets, we were in for at least two inches.

As Josh guided the van through bumper-high water on the way to La Crescenta, we passed the Los Angeles River. Most people know it as the dry concrete channel that is the backdrop for dozens of movie car chases. But this stretch of the river actually has an earthen bottom and was brimming with gray, rushing water and debris.

A green haze in the current caught my attention—a jade-green blur. I blinked my eyes and peered out the rain-soaked window to see whether I was imagining it. But something was definitely moving in the water. Someone.

"Stop," I shrieked. "Someone's in the river."

Josh slammed on the brakes, but in the rain, the van slid ten feet before coming to a stop. A car behind us honked, but Josh was unfazed. Without breaking a sweat, he angled the van out of traffic and to the side of the road.

"Call 911," I said, then grabbed my binoculars and jumped out of the van. The cold rain pelted me like a thousand tiny needles. I ran to the railing and looked over. The blur in the water was gone.

Damn. Had I imagined it? I ran in the direction the water was flowing. That's when I saw the green blur farther downstream. But it wasn't a blur anymore. With my binoculars, I could make out that it was a teenage girl in a green sweatshirt in the midst of the rushing waters.

I ran the length of the chain-link fence, trying to find a way down to the river, but the only gate I found was locked. I pulled the rain-sopped hair away from my eyes and shook the gate to no avail. Where were the rescuers?

Then I noticed a small section of chain link that was bent backward, forming a small opening. A child could have easily squeezed through, but an adult in an oversize rain jacket would have a hard time.

I stopped, stared at the twisted metal, and decided to wait for the rescue squad.

Help her, I thought.

But what could I do? I wasn't experienced in first aid and didn't have even a vague idea what to do if I could get to her.

No one helped you when you were drowning. Don't repeat their mistake. Do something.

I dropped to my knees and slowly guided myself through the small opening. My coat snagged on the exposed wire a few times, but in less than a minute I was safely through.

A flat, grassy area extended about thirty feet and ended at a concrete embankment that led down to the river. The embankment was steep—at least a forty-five-degree angle.

I called out to the girl, but I could barely hear my own voice over the din of the rushing river. I stared at the water, trying to decide what to do. My legs felt like they'd been nailed to the ground.

Every second matters.

Slowly and steadily, I stepped down the wet concrete embankment, grateful that at least I'd had the foresight to wear sensible shoes. I still wasn't sure what I would do if I made it down to the water. One foot after another, I got closer to the churning waters below.

I kept shouting, trying to get her attention. When I got to the edge, she turned toward me, her eyes glassy, her face scratched and swollen, her lips trembling. I stumbled, slipping down the embankment.

Then I was in the river. The shock of the cold water took my breath away. I clawed at the embankment, which was only feet away, but the current was strong, and it dragged me downstream, away from the side.

I panicked. Eric's one swimming lesson hadn't prepared me for the deep end of a pool, much less this churning water. The water was about to claim me again.

Suddenly a tree limb slammed like a battering ram into my back, sending searing hot pain through my body. Its branches scraped the backs of my legs and entangled my feet as I struggled to pull away. My head slid under, and water rushed into my ears and up my nose as the swift current carried me downstream.

Thrashing my arms wildly, I used every fiber of strength I had left to push my head above water. I gasped, taking in air with the cold water. I shouted for help, but the pounding rain and rushing water drowned out my frail voice. I turned to see if the girl was still there, but I was easily two hundred yards from where I'd fallen in, and I could only see the endless gray of the falling rain.

Ahead I saw what appeared to be a narrow patch of concrete across the channel. I felt a brief glimmer of hope. Did the river end here? But my hope evaporated when I realized it was a low-head dam, a narrow concrete cap that drops the flowing water into a deep basin designed to slow down the water.

As I neared the dam, all I could see was a churning line of white water and the horizon. I tried to find anything to grab on to, to slow me down, but the swift current kept pushing me closer. My body scraped along the edge and stayed there for a moment before the force of the water pushed me over.

It felt as though I were falling forever. All I could see was the rolling water below, and then I hit it with a force that knocked the wind out of me. I plunged underwater, my body tumbling in every direction to the point where I didn't know which way was up. I was forced to the bottom, debris ripping at my skin.

I saw the few remaining bubbles escape my mouth. Then there was no more air. No more bubbles. Everything became blurry and slow.

The turbulent current pushed me to the surface then. But before I could catch my breath, I was dragged under again, sucked into what felt like an endless whirlpool. The water pressed against my eyes and rushed up my nose, stealing my breath with its bitter coldness. I tumbled again, unable to get my head above the rolling water, my body leaden and heavy. Sharp pain pierced my lungs and ripped through my body.

Something grabbed hold of my arm and dragged me. Then everything went black.

My chest was rocking with spasms. I heard a loud wheezing sound and realized it was coming from my throat. I coughed then felt water rise from within me and out of my mouth. Everything went white in front of my eyes.

Then something hard and plastic was placed over my mouth and nose, and warm air rushed into my lungs. I opened my eyes and found myself staring up at a man with blue eyes and rusty hair, cropped short.

"Can you hear me? Don't try to talk. Just nod your head."

I nodded my head slightly and became aware of a loud droning around me.

"She's awake," he said.

I was in a helicopter. And I was alive. There were heavy warm blankets on me. Still, my teeth were chattering and my body was shaking violently.

"Pulse is steady. BP normal. Body temp is ninety-six but rising," he said into his headset.

I felt the drowsiness pull me back in, and I closed my eyes, surrendering to it. Moments later I felt a warm hand stroking my hair, soothing me with its gentle touch. Was this standard paramedic treatment?

I opened my eyes expecting to see the red-haired guy, but instead it was Eric looking at me, wearing a wetsuit, his hair soaking wet.

"Don't try to talk," he said gently. "We're taking you to Burbank Hospital. We got the girl, too," he said, as though reading my mind.

I felt a surge of relief as he continued to stroke my hair. Just looking at him comforted me. "You've got scrapes and bruises, but you'll pull through this fine."

"Thanks to this one," the redheaded paramedic said, nodding toward Eric. "He was the one who pulled you out."

"We all did it," Eric said.

I couldn't have spoken if I'd wanted to. All I could do was look at him. The water had tried to claim me again, just as I thought it would. But it failed—defeated at the last moment by Eric, who had torn me from its grasp.

He stopped stroking my hair and took my hand. His hand was hot—as if it was on fire—and I gripped it tightly.

"They call that a drowning machine," he said quietly. "It sucks you into it, and it's nearly impossible to get out, even for the most experienced swimmer. But you made it. Maybe your swimming lesson paid off."

Even through his smile, I saw that his eyes were shaded with worry. Then a curtain of sleep began its descent on me, and I closed my eyes.

"I miss you." He said it so softly that I had no doubt it was genuine.

I opened my eyes and met his gaze, wondering why I had let Jack and the Good Sam story get between us.

Time moves differently in a hospital. In the outside world, everyone is rushing, stressing, planning, strategizing, pushing on to the next appointment and the next thing. Inside, time slows like pulled taffy. In the hushed quiet of the hospital, everyone waits. For test results. For the doctor. For good news.

After twenty-four hours that seemed to stretch on for weeks, the doctor finally gave me the news. His words came at me in a blur. I had aspirated water, but my lungs were clear. I hadn't gone into respiratory or cardiac arrest. They were treating me for hypothermia and exhaustion.

I could attest to the exhaustion: a simple walk from the hospital bathroom to the bed felt like climbing Everest. I was too tired to eat, and when the nurses turned on the TV news for me, I nodded off after three minutes.

Forty-eight hours later, I finally felt the haze lift. I showered, washed my hair for the first time in days, and managed to gulp down a few bites of the powdered scrambled eggs the nurse had brought, along with some kind of good-for-you pink fluid that tasted like chalk.

I heard a knock at the door and expected to see the nurse coming to cajole me into drinking more of the pink fluid. Instead, Eric entered the room dressed in his crisp navy blue uniform and carrying a Starbucks coffee.

We looked at each other for a moment, and neither of us said a word. On impulse, I hugged him. I felt his arms briefly wrap around me, but a moment later, he released me.

He placed the cup on the tray table next to my scrambled eggs. "Black. One sugar. I'm willing to bet it's better than anything they're serving in here. Although it may be too hot outside for you to drink it. We're having a heat wave."

I glanced out the window. People who don't live here think Southern California weather is boring in its sameness, but it often seems fickle and unpredictable to me. One day you can get caught in a downpour, and there can be flash floods; the next day can be eighty degrees and balmy.

"I just spoke with one of the doctors, and she said you're going to come through this fine."

I nodded. "They're going to release me later today."

He looked at the ground for a moment. "Well, I need to get going," he said. "I just wanted to check and make sure you were okay."

He'd been in the room for sixty seconds and was already preparing to leave. I looked at him, confused. The feelings he had expressed in the helicopter seemed to have completely evaporated.

"In the helicopter," I said. "You said something that—"

"That was in the heat of the moment," he said abruptly. He shifted his weight to his other leg. Like he couldn't wait to get out of there. "Then I went home that night and saw you and your Good Sam—now congressional candidate—splashed all over the news, and I realized you were never really honest about your feelings about him. It was always him. And always will be."

I was about to reply when the door swung open again and my dad hurried into the room. "Katie!" he said. "Sorry it took so long to get here. My flight was delayed because of that damn storm."

When he saw Eric, my dad stopped and, without missing a beat, extended his hand. "Hello there. I'm Hale Bradley, Kate's father."

"Eric Hayes."

"Eric is the firefighter who pulled me out of the water."

My dad's face brightened. "It's a pleasure to meet you, Eric. Thank you for rescuing my daughter. She's a brave one, going out into that river after that young girl, but from what I saw on the news, you were even braver. I can't thank you enough for risking your life to pull her out."

"It's what we're here for," Eric said, clearly uncomfortable with my dad's praise.

My dad placed a carefully wrapped present in front of me on the bed. "A late birthday present," he said. "You know, Eric, she's the last person I'd ever think would need rescuing. Since she was little, she always wanted to do everything herself. Always *could do* everything herself." He turned to me. "Katie, I think this may be the first time you've been in a situation where you actually needed someone else to help you out."

There was some truth to what he said, and it's why I wanted to put the whole event behind me. I didn't like needing Eric. I didn't like thinking that if he hadn't been there when he had, I might not be living and breathing today. Worse, I was embarrassed that my dad was saying all this in front of Eric, especially when it was obvious Eric was looking for any opportunity to leave.

"They're playing the story over and over on your Channel Eleven," my dad said, switching on the TV.

I frowned. I didn't like the idea of being the *subject* of a news report, especially where I was the one being rescued. "They probably titled the story 'The Worst Way to Save a Drowning Person,'" I said with a laugh, trying to hide my embarrassment. "I'm sure they're pointing out all the reasons I shouldn't have gone after her."

"You did the right thing," Eric said. "You should be proud of that."

I eyed him over the rim of my Starbucks cup. "All I ended up doing was make you have to rescue *two* people instead of one. I should have stayed in the van and waited for the rescuers. I never got near enough to be of any help to her."

"She was losing consciousness, and apparently all your shouting at her kept her awake," he said. "She's telling everyone that the two of us saved her life."

I liked the way he said "the two of us" and smiled at him, but he looked away.

My dad, however, was beaming. "Eric, let us take you to dinner to thank you. It's the least we can do."

"That's very generous of you. But unfortunately I can't. And I need to get going." He extended his hand to my father. "It was a pleasure to meet you, Senator Bradley."

He headed to the door without even a glance in my direction. The door clicked behind him, and suddenly I felt drained and weak, as though he had taken all my energy with him. A hollow lump formed in the pit of my stomach as I realized I would probably never see him again.

My dad sat on the bed next to me. "Jack called me to say he'll be back in LA tomorrow," he said. "He's sorry he couldn't be here with you."

It was so like Jack to make a show of his concern for me to my father but not even bother to contact me. "I need to ask you something about Jack's campaign."

"Slow down a little for once, Katie. There'll be plenty of time later to talk about Jack and his campaign. When you're feeling better."

"I'm feeling well enough." I lied. "When did he first start talking to you about running for Congress?"

"When hasn't he talked to me about running for office?" he said smiling. Then, seeing my serious expression, he sobered. "We began discussing the thirty-third congressional district race in detail about two months ago."

Two months ago. Jack had sworn he didn't plan his candidacy until after he gave away the money as Good Sam. *Another lie.*

"Why did he choose the thirty-third district?"

"The incumbent, Charles Campbell, is a good friend of mine. Charles had announced he wasn't going to run again, and Jack asked me whether I thought he had a shot at getting the seat."

"You must have said yes."

"Of course I said no," he said. "Jack is very bright and well connected, but he didn't have the name recognition or the track record to run for that seat. It's a very competitive district. The men who've held that seat had been household names because of other positions they'd held and Jack really didn't have that. Not then anyway."

I took a gulp of the pink fluid and resisted the urge to gag. "It looks to me like he manufactured the Good Sam event in order to get that name recognition."

"Ah, your skepticism is showing." He brushed the sleeves of his navy blue pinstripe suit. "He says the two are unrelated and I do believe him. I can tell you this, though. From what Jack says, the best outcome of his Good Sam generosity was not that he got all the recognition but that it got the two of you back together."

I frowned. "We're not back together."

"That's not what he's thinking." He stretched his arms over his head. "But after meeting Eric, I can see why you don't share that same goal."

I shot him a quizzical look.

"I'm don't usually pay attention to such things, but even I can see that there's something important going on between you two."

I felt my cheeks turn pink. My dad had never been one to talk much about relationships, even when I was a teenager going on my first dates, so this was new territory for the two of us. "I know this is going to be hard to believe, but for once in your life, you're not right," I said with a grin. "There isn't anything between Eric and me. Ever since I started working with Jack on Good Sam, Eric will hardly even speak to me."

He laid a big hand on mine. "The Katie I raised would never let anyone refuse to talk with her. And the reporter I know would chase that person down and ask questions until she got the answers she wanted."

He was right. If this were a news story, I would pursue Eric as though he were a reluctant interview subject and ask questions until I got answers.

But this wasn't a news story. And while every instinct told me the feelings Eric shared in the helicopter were real, what could I really do?

My dad drove me home from the hospital and left an hour later after pressing five hundred dollars in my hand and urging me to "splurge a little." I think he meant for me to spend it on a mini shopping spree at some point, but the only splurge I imagined was an all-day massage to work the spasms out of my lower back and neck.

I spent the next twenty-four hours trying to figure out the rigorous regimen the doctors and nurses had prescribed. The pills, the ointments, and the sheaf of papers outlining detailed instructions covered my entire kitchen table. It looked like it would be a full-time job to follow all of them.

But while my body was in recovery mode, my heart was undergoing a separate restoration. Several times I picked up my cell phone and punched in Eric's number, but each time I went to press the green "Call" button, I set the phone aside instead.

I tried to distract myself from thinking about him by catching up on the news, making sure I read, not just skimmed, all the stories our interns had compiled from sources around the globe. But inevitably I lost focus, and the next thing I knew, I was staring out the window instead.

I was never a daydreamer as a kid, and certainly not as an adult, so I wasn't used to being this unproductive. I threw on some clothes, swept a little makeup across my face, and headed to Eric's house. Every step of the way I knew that my plan was poorly thought-out. But I had resolved to treat this like any news story I pursued. I needed to get answers.

As I got closer to his house, I became more nervous about my decision and considered turning back. My hand trembled as I lifted the brass sailboat knocker on his front door. Pain now shot through my neck and shoulders, and I battled the urge to tear up. I wasn't ready for this. I should've waited until I had recovered. Until I had a better plan.

Then the door swung open, and Eric was standing in the doorway. Like the first time I'd met him, I was momentarily speechless.

"What you said in the helicopter," I said hoarsely. "That was real."

He looked at me for a beat, but I couldn't tell from his expression what he was thinking. "Let's get you off your feet."

I stepped inside and sat on Eric's couch, unsure of what to do next. He sat next to me, dressed now in dark jeans and a black V-neck T-shirt. Wow, did he look good. When you've been sick for even a little while and then get well enough to rejoin the world of the healthy, everything seems strange yet somehow more magnificent. Colors are brighter, sounds are more vivid, and you feel like you're experiencing them anew.

"Jack and I are not together," I said. "It may look like it on TV, but that's just Jack manipulating things. What Jack wants is to become the congressional representative of the thirty-third district of California."

"I know what Jack wants. But what do you want?"

His question caught me off guard. I had come here to ask questions, not answer them. I rubbed my sore neck, trying to rehearse an answer in my head, but the words came out before I could think them through. "When Jack came forward as Good Sam, I admit, I did have feelings for him at first. He was the very person I had been searching for. Someone I didn't think existed. He was generous, doing extraordinary good, and he was doing it anonymously without expecting any reward. I had fallen for a story. I was in love with Good Sam."

He considered my words for a moment. "You didn't answer the question," he said finally. "What do *you* want?"

I shifted in my seat. I was rarely on the receiving end of a question. Certainly not one this big. I drew a deep breath, steeling myself for the courage to answer it. "I want . . . you. The way it was between us."

At first, I wasn't sure he heard me. He was staring at one of the sailboat paintings on the wall across the room. I couldn't tell what he was thinking, and as each second ticked by, I kicked myself for saying too much.

I stood and headed to the door. Given his silence, it seemed the only thing to do. "I realize I never thanked you. For rescuing me from the drowning machine."

He stood, his gaze now focused on me. "Maybe you've been the one rescuing me."

Eric certainly didn't look like someone who needed rescuing—certainly not by me anyway. But for the first time, I caught a glimpse of pain behind his eyes. Something I hadn't seen before, nor did I understand.

"I'm pretty sure I was the one stuck in the drowning machine, not you."

His expression softened. "I think I've been stuck in a drowning machine of my own for far too long," he said, slowly crossing the room toward me. "Until I met you."

I didn't know what he meant by that and I didn't care, because the way he was looking at me then, his eyes lingering on my face as though he were memorizing every detail, was all that really mattered.

"Don't go," he whispered, then braced an arm against the wall behind me and leaned in close. I felt the cool fabric of his shirt graze my skin. Then he lowered his mouth to mine in a kiss that was soft at first, tender and sweet, turning every aching muscle in my body into warm honey.

As the sun began its slow descent behind the slate-gray mountains, the soft afternoon air turned cool. Eric headed into the kitchen to make me some chicken soup.

"Not from a can or a box," he promised.

I'd never made chicken soup from scratch, and certainly never had seen a guy do it, either. But his years in the fire department clearly had made him comfortable in the kitchen. He moved swiftly, not a single motion wasted, grabbing what he needed, chopping and dropping it into a cast iron pot.

In my experience, when a guy cooks for a woman, he does it as a surefire seduction ploy—a way to make her feel cared for and relaxed, and maybe to show off a little so he can whisk her off to bed later. If that was his intention, it was working. After a little wine, I felt the aches in my muscles relaxing.

"You'll have to stop looking at me like that," he said, "or I won't finish making the soup."

"What kind of look am I giving you?" I said, all sassy and confident. But I was a bundle of nerves inside.

"Like you want me to kiss you."

"You misread my look, Captain Hayes," I whispered, bringing my lips within inches of his. "I was only marveling at your onion-chopping technique."

His eyes were smoky with laughter. "If I didn't have my hands full of onions, I'd kiss that grin off your face."

"Promises, promises," I said and slipped out of arm's reach.

In the corner of the pantry by the back door, I spotted something that resembled a two-foot-tall vinyl horseshoe.

"What's this?" I asked, peering at the faded orange cover, dry and cracked like peeling bark.

"A buoy. It used to be on my brother's boat. We had it since we were kids, but he thought it brought him good luck, so he made sure it was onboard every time he sailed."

"So everyone in your family liked to sail?"

"Brian loved sailing more than anything. He said it was in our blood because we had a great-grandfather who used to build ships. Brian was always the first to get on and the last to get off *The Crazy Eight*."

"*The Crazy Eight*?"

He dumped a handful of chopped onions into the pot. "That was the name of Brian's boat. She was fast but steady, even in choppy water. And beautiful. As elegant a mast as I've ever sailed."

"Do you have photos?"

"There's a photo album somewhere on the shelf in the living room."

I found the album nestled alongside *Navigation the Easy Way*, a worn copy of *Two Years Before the Mast*, and a tome titled *The Annapolis Book of Seamanship*. Inside was page after page of sailboat photographs, taken at sea at all times of the day and night. I could feel the photographer's love of sailing in the way the light caressed the tall sails and glinted on the deep blue waters. There were pictures of Brian and Eric sailing, both of them tanned and smiling. Other photos were of a party while the ship was moored in a marina—sun-kissed faces in the glow of warm lights, wineglasses raised.

One of the faces in the photographs looked familiar. I leaned in to get a closer look. Standing on deck, his arms linked with Brian's and Eric's, was Larry Durham, the out-of-work carpenter who had received money from Good Sam—or at least someone who looked like him. Maybe it was an optical illusion. Perhaps at the precise moment the photograph had been taken, the light and shadows had assembled in such a way as to make the man look like Larry Durham.

I brought the photo album into the kitchen. "Is this Larry Durham?"

Eric peered over my shoulder at the photo. "Not sure who it is."

"He looks exactly like one of the people I interviewed who received money from Good Sam." I noticed the tattoo on his neck. "Even down to the tattoo."

Eric shook his head. "I think he was a friend of my brother's. From New Jersey."

"Weird how the eyes can play tricks on you."

Eric placed a warm hand around my waist, nuzzled my neck, and took the album from my hands. "Why don't you put that book away and taste this chicken soup? I think it's missing something."

Maybe it was his touch that crackled like electricity along my skin or the way he toyed with my feet under the table as I inhaled the delicious soup he had made. Maybe it was the way he spoke to me, caressing me with his voice, deep and warm. It felt right being with him, like we always had been together. Yet there was also a tension between us.

I think we both felt our attraction deepening but weren't sure what we were going to do about it.

"Have your eyes always been green?" he asked.

"I'm never going to live that down, am I?"

A soft grin lifted the corners of his mouth. "I kind of liked it—your coming on to me like that."

"I wasn't coming on to you," I said. "I really thought your eyes were green."

I picked up my bowl and headed to the kitchen. As I passed him, he reached out and tugged on my hand.

"You weren't flirting with me then? Not even a little?"

"Not even a little," I said, teasing. "I hardly noticed you."

He stood. "And now? Would you flirt with me now?"

"Maybe a little," I whispered, as my pulse picked up its pace.

He kissed me, more urgently this time. I felt his body, rigid and hard against mine, and I knew where this was headed, knew where I wanted it to go. My hand lingered at his waist then roamed the length of his body, pulling him to me.

He closed his eyes. "Don't," he whispered, "or I won't be able to keep my promise to be a Boy Scout tonight."

"I don't remember your promising to be a Boy Scout." I said it brazenly, but I was quaking inside, anticipating what would come next, surprised by my own need.

He took my hand and held it. "God, I want this," he said quietly. "I want you."

I drank in what he said, absorbed it like a thirsty flower in a desert rain. I was supposed to be the one with a gift for words, but in that moment, I didn't have any.

He pressed a kiss to my forehead. "But given what you've been through, we shouldn't rush things."

I linked my arms around his neck. "I'm fine. Really I am."

"You almost drowned. You need to rest, get your strength back."

He'd said it gently, sincerely. I had no doubt he was concerned about me. Still I couldn't help feeling stung by his rejection. Most men would've seized the opportunity no matter what a woman had been through—especially when I was so clearly willing. But Eric was not most men.

It only made me want him more intensely. As I lay on the couch with him, his arms enfolding me, I felt wonderfully cared for, safe. But as my eyes grew heavy, I wondered what it would be like to touch his body freely. To have him touch me. What it would be like when we finally made love.

CHAPTER FOURTEEN

"I'm fine." I argued on the phone with David the next morning. I had finished my third cup of coffee and was organizing all the medicines on my kitchen table, getting a little stir-crazy.

"You almost drowned. Seriously, take a few more days off and come back when you're one hundred percent better."

"I *am* one hundred percent better. Want to call my doctor? He'll tell you." I was bluffing, of course, because I hadn't seen my doctor since I'd been released from the hospital.

He sighed. "All right. But I'm giving you an easy assignment."

"But—"

"Don't argue," he protested. "Take it easy. When you're up for it, I want you to get reaction from a Good Sam recipient about Jack Hansen's bid for Congress."

"On it. Who's already been interviewed?"

I heard him clicking through a list on his computer. "Just about all of them. But no network or station has been able to get Dr. Kryvoskya or that Durham guy to talk to them on camera. But seeing as you broke the story with them, maybe they'll talk to you. So pick one of them, but only one today. Then go home and rest. I mean it, Kate. Go slow."

I wasn't interested in going slow. I wanted to race back into my life. Unfortunately, my body wasn't cooperating. The muscles in my legs and back, bruised and battered, pulsed with hot pain. I figured the best way to get through the rest of it was to forge ahead and get my mind off it.

Josh had been assigned to cover a story about the Valley Bandits, who had just pulled off their third bank robbery in the San Fernando Valley, so the newsroom assigned a new cameraman, Jeff, to work with me for the day. I was disappointed but also relieved. Jeff was a thirtysomething cameraman with two awards for video photojournalism from the National Press Photographers Association, so I knew his work would be good. I had also heard that he wasn't one for small talk, which meant I wouldn't have to expend any energy holding a conversation.

As I left my apartment and headed to the waiting news van, I was surprised to find Alex waiting for me. His normally pressed khakis were wrinkled, and it actually looked like he had the beginnings of a five o'clock shadow on his pale young face. "I know you're still recovering from the accident but . . . how do I say this?" He ran his fingers through his mussed hair. "I haven't told anyone. And I didn't want to tell you over the phone or in front of everybody. I've been waiting until you were well enough—"

"What's this about, Alex?"

"Phil, the forensics accountant, put together a detailed list of each of Jack's cash withdrawals." He paused, clearly nervous. "It looks like Jack definitely withdrew over a million dollars, like he said he did. But we followed the money and . . ." He trailed off.

"Go on," I urged.

"Jack's first withdrawal of funds happened two days *after* Michael and Marie Ellis received their cash. The money they received didn't come from Jack Hansen."

I felt my skin get clammy. "Why the hell didn't Phil tell us this before?"

"Jack sent something like eight different statements with more than one hundred transactions in a thirty-day period. If you remember, Phil verified that Jack had withdrawn more than a million dollars, but we hadn't hired him to correlate the dates people received money with the actual withdrawals."

I leaned against the van to steady myself. "But if he didn't withdraw the money until two days after the Ellises got their cash from Good Sam, then how did they or Cristina Gomez or Larry Durham or even Dr. K get their money?"

"Phil and I have been wondering the same thing," he said quietly. *Was it possible that Jack wasn't Good Sam?*

If Jack wasn't Good Sam, then who was?

I turned this question over and over in my mind as Jeff drove me through Hollywood that morning. There's an otherworldly quality to every neighborhood in the early-morning hours, and Hollywood is no exception. Its graffiti-stained sidewalks and front yards fortressed with chain-link fences were awash with sleep and an almost luminous greenish-yellow light. The sounds of the city in the distance were hushed, while the ones up close were magnified—the hiss of sprinklers, the sparrows calling out from the eucalyptus trees.

"Where do you want to go first?" Jeff asked as we stopped at a busy intersection.

I handed him the scribbled piece of paper with the addresses David had given me for Dr. Kryvoskya and Larry Durham. "Let's start with Larry Durham," I said absently, then turned my attention to a large black crow preening on a bus stop bench. He marched along the bench, ruffling his feathers and trumpeting a steady caw.

While Jack had paraded himself as Good Sam, was the real Good Sam still out there, still undiscovered?

I needed time to think this through and wished I hadn't agreed to take on today's assignment.

"This is 144 North Mariposa," Jeff said, interrupting my thoughts. "Larry Durham's house."

As he parked the van, I spotted Larry Durham going into his front door. I got out, gingerly favoring my right leg, which was stiffer than the other.

"Larry!" I called out. "Wait!"

I'm sure I was quite the sight, hobbling toward him, shouting.

"Shouldn't you be at home recovering? I saw the story about you getting caught in the river."

"News never sleeps." I shuffled up the steps, surprised how much out of breath I was after such a short distance. "I'm trying to get reactions to Good Sam's run for Congress."

"Much as I like getting the money, I kind of wish Good Sam hadn't come." He swept a cobweb from his entryway. "Complete strangers call or just show up on my doorstep asking for money. New 'friends' invite me to stuff, hoping I'll pick up the tab or invest in one of their dreams. And you reporters never leave me alone."

"How do you feel about Jack Hansen—Good Sam—running for public office?"

He shrugged. "I like that he's looking out for guys like me. Can't say that most politicians even take notice."

"Can I get you to say that on camera?"

He pulled a pack of cigarettes out of his back pocket. "You know I won't. So you can stop asking."

"It'll only take a minute to—"

"Don't waste your time on me." He touched a lighter to the end of the cigarette and started to go back into his house. "Go on. Interview someone else."

I could tell from the way he was looking at me that I wouldn't be able to persuade him to agree to an interview this time. But then I remembered the photo I'd seen in Eric's album. The image that looked like Larry Durham. "You got a twin, Larry?" I asked, hoping the questioning might keep him talking long enough that I could get him to change his mind about an interview.

He stopped and turned around. "Not that my parents told me."

"Funny thing. Someone was showing me some photographs and I swear I saw someone who looked exactly like you."

He shrugged. "Maybe it was me."

"You ever been on a sailboat that belonged to Brian and Eric Hayes?"

He blew a cloud of smoke out of the corner of his mouth. "All the time."

The blood drained from my face. I struggled for words, but nothing came out of my mouth.

"Why are you looking at me like that? I don't look like the boating kind to you? You think because I don't wear Top-Siders and khakis, I can't set foot on a sailboat?"

"It's not that. I didn't expect you to know Eric or Brian."

"Know them? I was practically a member of their family."

"How did you know them?"

His eyes narrowed. "You doing a story about them?"

I shook my head.

"Brian was my best friend since fourth grade. After high school we kind of went our separate ways. He became big with the whole houses thing, while I went to work with my hands, building houses. But the boats always brought us back together. I did all the repairs to the decks and a good load of the cabinetry below."

"Eric said it wasn't you in the photograph on the sailboat."

"Can't blame him for forgetting, considering what he's been through."

I raised an eyebrow. "What do you mean?"

"The accident. It devastated everyone—Eric more so than just about anyone."

I didn't know what he meant about an accident, but I knew better than to press too hard. "How do you mean?"

"He shut down after that. He'd not only lost a brother, but he lost his sailing buddy, the one person who loved sailing almost as much as he did."

"Do you still see him?"

"Eric? No. I think I remind him too much of the times we had when Brian was alive." He lowered his voice to a near whisper. "Good times."

Larry looked away and turned silent after that. His solemn expression made me reconsider asking any more questions.

My mind was racing, but I knew what I had to do next. Maybe Larry's connection to Eric and Brian Hayes was just a coincidence, a fluke. So we headed to Cristina Gomez's house to test my theory. Unfortunately, Jeff didn't have Josh's navigating skills, so we got lost twice before we finally found her place.

Cristina Gomez had become one of Jack Hansen's biggest supporters. She had seen and read everything about his run for Congress and seemingly memorized it, reciting it nearly word for word. Sporting a new haircut that made her look ten years younger, she spoke with me on her front porch.

"We need a congressman like Jack Hansen. He will make the needs of workers like me a priority."

She went on in detail about how Jack Hansen had changed her life, but I wasn't listening. I was wondering why Eric hadn't told me anything about his brother's accident. Why had he never mentioned he knew Larry Durham, even when I talked about the people Good Sam had helped? Even when Larry was in the photograph with Eric and Brian?

Then my mind made one of those giant leaps it often does when facts and evidence don't make sense. Forget Occam's razor, the theory of the fourteenth-century philosopher that the simplest answer is most often the correct one. Sometimes the most far-fetched answer is the only plausible one.

A far-fetched question for Cristina Gomez was poised on my tongue. A wave of heat rushed to my head as I waited for the right time to ask it.

When Cristina paused for a moment, the question flew out of my mouth. "Did you know a man named Brian Hayes?"

I expected her to look at me strangely, maybe even to ask what this question had to do with the interview about Jack Hansen. Instead her eyes misted over. "Of course."

My throat tightened. I had my answer. But what now?

"How did you know him?" I asked.

"I was a babysitter to his son from when he was born until he started school last year. Why do you ask about him?"

"It's complicated," I said, unsure how to explain my thinking. "Did you know him very well?"

"I used to babysit his son every day and sometimes until late into the night. Brian and his wife worked long hours. The boy, Jonathan, was often sick. He had many ear infections, pneumonia twice . . . and terrible asthma."

Was it simply an odd coincidence that two of the people Jack had given money to had connections to Brian Hayes? Was it possible that if I interviewed people at random—say, two people in the grocery checkout line—I could find something that linked them together?

I remembered the words of one of my college journalism professors. "The problem with being human is that we see connections to events that are purely coincidental. What you need is proof."

I was going to find it.

∽

Robert Kryvoskya, also known as Dr. K, closed the door in my face when I went to his home. I rang the doorbell again, my mind racing to figure out what to say if he reopened it.

He flung it open and started speaking before he even saw me. "I appreciate your persistence, but I won't discuss my political views on television. You're the third reporter this week to ask me about Jack Hansen, and quite frankly I'm fed up with the constant intrusion." He started to close the door again.

"I have only one question." I gave him my most sincere look. "One that isn't political or about Jack Hansen."

He raised an eyebrow and spoke in a tone I'm sure he usually reserved for recalcitrant students. "What would that be?"

I exhaled sharply, steeling my nerves. "I want to ask you about Brian Hayes."

His tone softened. "What about him?"

"Did you know him?"

"Of course," he said.

"How did you know him?"

He glanced around me. I guessed he wanted to see if there was a camera pointed at him. There wasn't.

A smile tipped the corners of his mouth, and his eyes brightened. "Brian started in the entrepreneur program at UCLA about five years ago, after a couple of years selling real estate. He was making quite a lot of money already in the real estate business, but he knew he couldn't advance to the next level unless he branched out and went on his own."

"He started his own business?"

Dr. K nodded. "Within two years his firm was the fourth-largest real estate buyer in Los Angeles. He did remarkably well in a short time."

"He learned how to do it from you?"

"I can't take credit for that. Brian already had a lot of the skills he needed to be a successful entrepreneur before coming into my program. What he lacked was confidence in his ability to go out on his own. Perhaps, in a small way, I helped him find his confidence."

"How did you do that?"

He beamed with pride. "I suppose the answer you're expecting is that I imparted some dense wisdom gained from a textbook. But it wasn't that way. Brian came to see me after he graduated from the program. He was struggling with some fairly significant business issues, and his investors and advisers were urging him to go in a direction he wasn't comfortable with. He asked me what to do, and I said, 'You already know the answer. You have everything you need to make this decision.' Brian thanked me later, even credited me with catapulting his business to the top, although I can't say I did much of anything."

"Did he ever—"

"Why are you asking about Brian Hayes?" He interrupted.

I felt my mouth go dry. "That's a very good question," I said, almost to myself. "What would you think if I told you that at least three of the people who received money from Good Sam all knew Brian Hayes?"

Dr. K considered that for a moment and straightened his bow tie. "I'd think it was an interesting coincidence but nothing more. I don't know if you're aware, but Brian Hayes is dead."

"Yes, I know."

"When Brian was alive, he knew a lot of people. He was very outgoing and had many friends. Had to be in his line of work. That some of them later received money from Jack Hansen is odd, but it's still a coincidence."

I wasn't buying the coincidence angle, even though I wanted to. But if it wasn't a coincidence, what was it? Why did all of these people have connections to Brian Hayes? Was Eric somehow involved in all of this?

Dr. K must have sensed my skepticism. "Tell me . . . what are your father's initials?"

I tilted my head. "Why do you want to know?"

"Tell me your father's initials. I'll explain."

"HDB."

"Let's say that you go into an antique store, buy a watch, and return home to find the initials 'HDB' engraved on it. You'd say there was a connection of some sort. Surely not a coincidence. Am I right?"

"Right."

"But statistics will tell you that if everyone in Los Angeles were to buy an antique engraved watch, three thousand people would find their father's initials on it. Three thousand people. Call it luck, chance, randomness, coincidence. But that's what you've got here."

It made sense, but I wasn't convinced. After I left Dr. K's house, I dialed Jack's private cell phone, but it went to voice mail.

"I'm out of the hospital and back at work," I said after the beep. "Call me. There's something I have to ask you."

When Rob Haywood tried to deposit the one hundred thousand dollars he had received from Good Sam into his account at City National Bank, he asked the bank—begged, apparently—not to disclose his name to the press. But word leaked out to the Associated Press anyway, and Rob and his family were thrust into the media spotlight.

I had reported on Rob Haywood early on but didn't realize it. Turned out he was the anonymous caller who told me he'd received money with a note from Good Sam indicating the money was for his daughter, Lauren, to go to law school.

Rob's home looked like a cozy cottage the Seven Dwarfs might live in—wavy, uneven shingles on the rooftop, a red-brick chimney, and a meandering cobblestone path that led to the arched wooden front door.

I rang the doorbell, and soon after, a woman cracked open the front door and poked her head out. "I'm sorry, but we're not doing any interviews."

She started to close the door.

"I'm Kate Bradley from Channel Eleven. I only need a moment of your time."

"Please leave," she said through the door. "We don't want any more media attention."

"Did you know a man named Brian Hayes?"

"Yes," she said. She opened the door, so now I could see her entire body instead of just her head. She was dressed casually in a pair of skinny jeans and a plaid camp shirt. "Why do you ask? Are you doing a story about Brian Hayes?"

"We're considering it." I lied, hoping she didn't ask more questions. "How did you know him?"

"Brian was friends with my daughter Lauren in college."

"They dated?"

She shook her head. "Not like that. He was like a brother to her. She tutored him. That's how they met."

As accomplished as Brian Hayes sounded, I couldn't imagine he needed a tutor in college. "What did she tutor him in?"

"Everything. Most people didn't know it, but he had dyslexia. He was smart—very smart—but he had terrible trouble reading. No one thought he'd make it through college, but with Lauren's help, he did."

"And became very successful."

She nodded. "I don't think anyone ever expected that. Except Lauren. She always said he was going to go on and do great things."

All this new information was swirling around me, and my mind was frantically trying to make sense of it. My cell phone rang, adding to my confusion. I pulled it out of my purse and glanced at the screen. Jack Hansen.

I answered the call. "Jack, I'm in the middle of something. Can I call you back?"

"I really need to talk with you. It's important."

I covered the mouthpiece. "Sorry, I need to take this. Thank you for your time."

I left the Haywoods' front porch and started a slow walk back to the van.

"What's so important?" I asked.

"Sorry I didn't come to the hospital, but I had to fly to DC to meet with campaign advisers. I heard about your accident. You all right?"

"Better than I was a few days ago."

"They told me you went after a girl in the river, but I didn't believe it. Whatever possessed you to go in after her?"

"She was drowning, Jack."

He laughed. "Well, I'm sure you won't make the same mistake next time."

I wanted to tell him I was insulted by his comment, then I thought better of it. I didn't want him to know he could rattle me so easily.

"Let's have dinner tonight. I need your advice about my campaign."

I swallowed hard, shutting his dinner proposal out of my mind. "There's something I need to ask you. I want to know if . . . Did you know someone named Brian Hayes?"

"No. Should I?"

I surprised myself by rattling off facts about a man I never knew. "He owned a real estate firm in Los Angeles, loved sailing, had a wife and a kid named Jonathan."

"Doesn't ring a bell. But I've met so many people this last week, I can't remember everyone."

"He's dead." I paused dramatically. "He died about six months ago."

"Then why are you asking me about him?"

"At least four of the people you supposedly gave money to had some connection to Brian Hayes. And I wondered if you chose them because you knew him."

There was a long pause on the line. "Sounds like a strange coincidence—that's all. Someone with your high profile shouldn't waste time on such stuff when there's news of substance going on. I've just gotten endorsements from the Los Angeles Police Association and several key city council members. I want to talk to you over dinner and get some advice on how I should handle making these kinds of announcements."

"I can't make it, Jack. Gotta run—I have to take this other call."

There wasn't another call. I needed time to think this through. I wasn't surprised that Jack didn't know about the connections to Brian Hayes, because it confirmed what I already knew. Jack wasn't Good Sam.

But was Brian Hayes Good Sam? How could a man who died six months ago be doing this? And why?

John Baylor's house was my next stop. Before Jeff had brought the van to a complete stop, I slid out of the van, ignoring the shooting pain in my hips and legs. "I won't be long," I told him.

I spotted John Baylor on his front porch, peering at the screen of a silver laptop. Scowling, actually.

"Excuse me, Mr. Baylor," I called out. "I'm Kate Bradley from Channel Eleven. We met before."

"Yes, I remember."

"I'm sorry to bother you while you're working," I said, nodding toward the laptop.

He closed the laptop, set it aside, and stood. "I'm working on a story for *LA Weekly*, so any diversion from writing is a welcome distraction," he said with a twinkle in his eye. He shook my hand with a vigorous grip. "I'm guessing you're here about Good Sam."

"I'm supposed to be here to get your reaction to Jack Hansen—Good Sam—running for Congress. But that's not really what I'm looking for."

He looked puzzled. "Then why are you here?"

My throat tightened. "Did you know a man named Brian Hayes?"

He shook his head. "The name doesn't sound familiar. Should it?"

"Is it possible that your wife knew him?"

He shrugged. "Maybe. But why are you asking?"

"So far, all the people I've talked to who received money from Good Sam had some connection to him. I'm trying to figure out if it's a coincidence or a pattern."

The wind chimes on his porch tinkled in the light breeze. "Who is he?"

"He was in real estate. Owned a company called Residential Realty Trust. Maybe he sold you this house?"

He shook his head. "Never heard of him or his company. I inherited the house when my parents passed away several years ago."

I wasn't sure what to say. Was he mistaken? Lying?

"Could I ask your wife if she knew him?" Then I remembered that his wife was battling cancer. "On second thought—"

"She's up and about, so I'll ask her real quick." He headed to the front door. "We're leaving for Mayo tomorrow for the experimental treatment that Good Sam is helping us pursue."

As he went inside, I felt guilty for bothering him. Where was this line of questioning leading? Was it a wild-goose chase, or had I uncovered something I'd completely missed the first time around?

I was surprised then when John stepped back onto the porch and said, "My wife's never heard of Brian Hayes, either. We don't know anyone by the last name of Hayes. And the only real estate broker we know recently retired to Oregon."

I waited for what he said to sink in, but it just made my head hurt like one of those mind-bending math problems on the SAT. If Jack Hansen wasn't Good Sam and Brian Hayes was associated with some, but not all, of Good Sam's recipients, then who was Good Sam?

"You know, once we found out Jack Hansen was Good Sam, it all made sense," John said quietly.

I leaned against the porch railing. "How so?"

"Jack serves on the board of Human Rights Watch, where my wife works. I think he knew about her cancer and knew we've been struggling to make ends meet. So we understand why he chose us. And we're happy he's running for Congress. He deserves all the good that's coming to him."

I was more confused than ever. As I left John Baylor's house and headed back to the news van, the only theory that made sense was that Good Sam's connection to Brian Hayes was simply an odd set of coincidences. As Dr. K had pointed out, Brian had crossed paths with a lot of people in his lifetime, so the likelihood of anyone knowing him was fairly high.

But if Jack Hansen wasn't Good Sam, and Good Sam's connection to people who knew Brian Hayes was a mere coincidence, then who was Good Sam?

Now a heavy blanket of exhaustion had descended over me. I'd missed at least two doses of the medicines I was supposed to take, and searing pain shot down the back of my legs. Worse, fatigue was dulling my thinking.

I tried to ignore the pain and instead asked Jeff to drop me off at Marie Ellis's home. I decided that if Marie didn't know Brian Hayes, I would put the whole thing aside as an unusual series of coincidences and go home and rest.

Marie answered the door dressed in a black satin gown. Her hair was styled in an updo, and unlike the last time I saw her, she was wearing makeup. Her transformation was so dramatic that for a moment I thought I'd come to the wrong address.

I extended my hand. "I'm Kate Bradley, Channel Eleven. We met before—"

"Hello again," she said, her tone polite but curt. "We're on our way out. How can I help you?"

"This will only take a moment," I said. "Did you know a man named Brian Hayes?"

She tilted her head. The question clearly seemed odd to her. "No, I don't know anyone named Brian Hayes."

It took a moment for me to absorb what she said. If she didn't know him, then this was all just a strange coincidence.

"Why are you asking about this person?"

"I'm talking to some of the people who received money from Good Sam—Jack Hansen—and in a strange coincidence, almost everyone knew Brian Hayes."

"We don't know him," she said.

"We don't know who?" a man in a tuxedo asked, stepping into the foyer.

With his dark hair graying at the temples and his boyish face complete with cleft chin, Michael Ellis looked like a cross between Dr. Kildare and Harrison Ford.

"Did you know a man named Brian Hayes?" I asked.

"Yes, I did," he said, adjusting one of his cuff links. "Why do you ask?"

"I'm investigating a connection between Brian Hayes and some of the people who received money from Good Sam."

"I don't understand . . . ," he said.

"How did you know Brian Hayes?"

"He was a patient."

"If I remember right, you're a neurosurgeon?"

He nodded.

"What did you see him for?"

"Brian Hayes's medical history is confidential, but I can tell you he had a serious medical condition and wasn't expected to recover, yet he did."

"When was he your patient?"

He looked up as though the answer were written on the ceiling. "Maybe six, seven years ago."

"And he never had problems with the . . . the condition after that?"

"After surgery, he had a complete recovery—very remarkable, to say the least."

I'd never met Brian Hayes, but I knew as much about his life as I did about my friends' lives.

He had loved sailing most of all. He had overcome dyslexia and his self-doubts to launch a highly successful real estate business. He was a man who had faced a serious medical condition and, with the help of a great doctor, beaten the odds. A man who had married and had a son. A man who had died in some kind of accident.

It was a compelling portrait of one man's life. But what did any of it have to do with Good Sam?

I gulped down the rest of my coffee. After another dose of the medicines, a hot shower, and a gloppy application of antibiotic cream, the soreness screaming through my body had settled into a dull ache.

"It doesn't make sense," I said aloud, then felt foolish because I was alone in my apartment. I once read somewhere that talking to yourself is a sign of intelligence, but I think it means you're becoming unhinged.

That's how I felt, too. Unsettled. Confused. I wrote out the facts, hoping to make sense of them:

Larry Durham—Brian Hayes's best friend
Cristina Gomez—nanny to Brian's son
Robert Kryvoskya—teacher; convinced Brian to start his own business
Lauren Haywood—tutored Brian in college because of his dyslexia
Michael Ellis—neurosurgeon who saved Brian's life
John Baylor—no connection

Everyone except John Baylor had a connection to Brian Hayes. Was this simply a coincidence, as Robert Kryvoskya suggested?

I already knew the answer.

CHAPTER FIFTEEN

I didn't know if Eric was working. He'd explained once how the three platoons rotate twenty-four-hour shifts throughout the month, but the schedule seemed as complicated as the IRS tax code, so I hadn't retained much of it.

I headed to his house instead. Before I could knock, he opened the door.

He hugged me tight and led me inside. "You look much better. Got a little more color in your face. How're you feeling?"

I kicked off my tight shoes, settled next to him on the couch, and rubbed my swollen feet. "I feel like I've just finished playing the Super Bowl," I admitted. "Definitely overdid it today."

He gave me a concerned look. "You weren't working, were you?"

"Yeah, I was. I was doing a follow-up on the Good Sam story today, and I turned up the oddest coincidences. It has to do with your brother, Brian."

His voice rose. "Brian?"

"Today I talked to six people who received money from Good Sam. And all but one knew your brother and had a relationship—a history—with him."

Eric fell silent. I pulled my notebook out of my purse and went on, detailing every person I interviewed and their relationship with Brian.

The longer I spoke, the more agitated Eric became. Midway through the list, he stood and wordlessly headed to the fireplace. He squatted and rearranged the logs on the grate even though there wasn't a fire burning.

That's when I knew with absolute certainty he was Good Sam.

"You're Good Sam, aren't you?" I said softly.

He was silent for a long moment, but even from the couch, I saw his chest quickly rise and fall. He rose slowly and stiffly, as though he were eighty years old. I never had seen him look like this, with deep creases around his eyes, his skin getting paler by the moment.

His voice was barely above a whisper. "I've lied to you, Kate. I'm really sorry." He looked away. "I gave away a total of five hundred thousand dollars to five people, and then Jack saw an opportunity and exploited it."

I felt a jolt of nervous adrenaline. "Were you two in this together?"

Eric shook his head. "No."

So many blurry thoughts careened through my head that I couldn't get hold of any of them—except the simple truth that Eric had lied to me.

My voice hissed with disbelief. "Why didn't you tell me? Why did you keep this from me all this time?"

He looked down at his hands. "I wasn't sure how to tell you."

His cheerless expression tugged at my heart, but my anger was already on full burn. "I reported that Jack was Good Sam, and you knew the whole time that he wasn't. Yet you never said anything. All along you were the one I was looking for. Did it give you some sort of smug satisfaction to know I hadn't figured out the truth?"

"It wasn't like that."

"Some reporter I am—deceived not once but twice. While I was exposing one man as Good Sam, the real one was lying about what he'd done."

He shook his head. "I wasn't—"

I stood. I had no idea what to do—walk out, shout, or break down and cry.

"Don't go," Eric said. He touched his hand gently to mine. "It's not what you think. Let me explain."

His voice sounded like a roar in my ears. And his touch, instead of calming me, made me remember in vivid detail the lies Jack had told me at our engagement party when I confronted him about his affair with his former girlfriend.

"Let me explain, Kate," Jack had said. "It's not what you think."

I tried to take a deep breath, but my chest felt tight and constricted, as if a boulder were sitting on it. A wave of nausea engulfed me.

I had trusted. And once again I'd been betrayed.

Without a word I headed out of Eric's front door and let it swing closed behind me.

The tears didn't fall until I got into my car. There, sitting alone behind the wheel, with the scent of night-blooming jasmine wafting through my open window, I let them spill out.

How could I have been so stupid? Was it something about me—the way I looked or a personality flaw of some kind—that made men comfortable deceiving me? Was I somehow responsible, attracting liars in some subtle way that I was completely unaware of?

I wiped the tears from my eyes and put the car in gear. In the short time I'd known Eric, nothing about him had made me suspect that I couldn't trust him or that he was a liar. So much for reporter's instinct. But I should have known better when it came to Jack. I knew firsthand what he was capable of.

How had Jack done it? How had he managed to convince me and many others that *he* was Good Sam?

I dialed Jack's cell phone. He picked it up on the second ring.

"I've been trying to reach you all night," he said softly.

"Is it too late for me to come over?" I asked, surprised by the perkiness in my voice.

"I was hoping you'd say that." I heard him grin through the telephone line.

◦⌐

Dressed in a tailored suit I guessed cost upward of two thousand dollars and a crisp white shirt open at the neck, Jack looked every bit the handsome candidate. But I was unmoved. I felt strangely powerful as I walked into his suite, oddly at ease, even though my heart was pounding so hard I felt like I was running the LA Marathon. I stood in the center of the room and surveyed the surroundings: soft candlelight, quiet music, a bottle of wine chilling in an ice bucket, oysters on the half shell. Jack certainly had the evening planned out, even if he had forgotten that I can't stand oysters. Even the smell of them nauseates me.

"When were you going to tell me you weren't Good Sam?" My tone was drained of any emotion.

He shot me a confused look. "What are you talking about?"

"I talked to the real Good Sam—the man who really gave the money away."

"Whoever you talked to is lying," Jack said. "I gave you proof."

"Did you?"

"This is crazy, Kate. You know I did it."

"You didn't tell me the whole story, did you, Jack? You left out a few things."

He looked me square in the eyes. "I've told you everything."

Jack was a great actor, especially when caught in a lie, but his performance skills were definitely off tonight.

"I don't think you have. I'm putting together a report revealing the truth about this whole thing, telling everyone you lied about being Good Sam."

His face blanched. "You're going to flush your career down the tubes over a story fabricated by some liar? You're smarter than that."

I closed my eyes. "Tell me the truth, Jack. For once in your life, tell it like it really happened."

"I don't know what's gotten into you tonight," he said, "but you're scaring me. Do I have to prove all over again that I'm Good Sam?"

I sat on the couch beside him. "You're not Good Sam," I said wearily. "You withdrew the money *after* the first recipients found the cash on their front porches."

He rubbed a hand against his brow and inhaled sharply. "Okay. Okay." He walked to the bar and poured himself a scotch on the rocks. "I'm responsible for the last five hundred thousand that was given away—Villegas, DeVault, Frierson, Caruso, and Baylor," he said quietly.

"And the rest?"

"Someone else gave that away. I don't know who."

"Someone else gave five hundred thousand dollars away, and you took credit for all of it."

"I didn't think he'd come forward. In fact I was pretty sure he wouldn't because he worked so hard to conceal his identity."

I blinked. "So you piggybacked on the idea and took credit for the whole thing."

"I'd never seen anything like the media attention this guy was getting. Everywhere I went, people were talking about Good Sam in a positive way I'd never heard them talk about anyone. *You* were talking about him. I thought if I continued where he left off, it would increase my visibility tenfold."

"Well, you got what you wanted."

My sarcasm was lost on him. "It turned out better than I'd expected. I gave away five hundred thousand dollars—the cost of a flight of TV ads—and got recognition and a reputation that no amount of money could buy."

"And it didn't bother you that you were deceiving people about what you'd done? That you were taking credit for money someone else had given away?"

He sat beside me again. "It's not like I didn't give away *any* money, Kate. I did give away five hundred thousand dollars."

"And took credit for more than that."

"You're looking at this too literally," he said, "as though I'm some sort of bad guy for taking advantage of an opportunity. What harm was done? Five people found windfalls on their front porches because of me, and as a result of my interview on television, the idea of Good Sam has spread around the country."

I shook my head. "You took credit for something you didn't do."

He shifted in his seat. "You say you talked to the real Good Sam?"

"Yes."

"Did he mind that I took the credit?" he asked.

I shrugged. "I have no idea."

"The way he was giving, taking extraordinary precautions not to be identified, I was sure he wasn't doing it for the publicity. I figured he didn't want anyone to know what he'd done."

I spoke slowly, making sure he heard every word. "Doesn't it bother you that you lied to *me*?"

"Sure it does, Kate. But for both of us, it was better to keep it a secret. Look at the mileage we've both gotten out of this story."

I stared at him in bewilderment. "That's what this is for you— mileage? The truth doesn't matter as long as you get what you want."

"We *both* got what we wanted."

I stood. "It'll all be meaningless once I report the truth about Good Sam."

Jack slammed his fist on the coffee table. "Don't be stupid. You'll detonate your career and drag me along with you. I've worked too hard for that to happen."

"So you want me to keep quiet about it and continue to report on Good Sam, all the while knowing the whole thing is a sham? I can't do that, Jack."

He took my hand in his. "We're in this together," he said softly. "If it'll make you happier, I'll give another five hundred grand away . . . just so I don't get credit for giving away more than I really did."

He smoothed my hair with his hand and pressed his forehead to mine. But his charm wasn't working. His calculations, his manipulations, his justifications—all of them sickened me. I saw him for what he truly was—a hollow, empty man who, in his search for fame and political success, had lost his sense of right and wrong . . . if he ever had it.

"I've missed you," he whispered. "Let me pour you a glass of wine, and I'll show you how much."

"Where is the line, Jack?" I was trembling now. "How do you know where the lie ends and the truth begins?"

For the second time that day, I walked out the door and let it close behind me.

CHAPTER SIXTEEN

David Dyal wasn't cooperating. "I know you say this is purely hypothetical, but the whole idea is impossible," he said, without looking up from his computer.

"I'm only asking . . . what if Jack Hansen turned out to have faked being Good Sam and someone else was the real thing?"

"That's my point," he said, peering over his reading glasses at me. "How could he have faked it? He had proof."

I sighed. "Pretend for a moment that he did fake it. What do you think would happen if we ran a story disclosing the truth?"

He closed his laptop and looked at me. "What's going on, Kate?"

"What would happen if our viewers found out Jack Hansen isn't Good Sam after all."

"You know what would happen?" Behind his frames, his eyes flashed black with anger. "Every media outlet across the country would rush to report the fraud, if only to get back at us for scooping them on this story. Our ratings would plummet; the station owners would investigate why our news credibility had been compromised, and everyone associated with the story would be canned. Hypothetically, of course."

"Well, that's pretty clear," I said drily.

David's assistant, Jennifer, popped her head into his office. "Two minutes until the assignment meeting." She dropped a folder on his desk. "These need your signature."

While he was momentarily distracted, I slipped out of his office.

"I want to talk more about this, Kate," he called after me, but I had already rounded the corner.

They say hindsight is twenty-twenty, but it's not true. Hindsight is something less than twenty-twenty, because our impressions of what happened after the fact are still colored by our emotions.

Even in hindsight I was having a hard time comprehending that Jack had planned the Good Sam charade to gain notoriety. But what I could see in hindsight was that Jack hadn't changed into Good Sam. He'd only sharpened his skills of deception and raised the stakes. Whereas once he had lied about his relationships with other women, now he lied about the lengths he would go to in order to win a seat in Congress.

Eric was another matter. He didn't strike me as the type to plan an elaborate hoax. And unlike Jack, I didn't think he was wealthy enough to throw that kind of money around. But maybe he was better off than I knew. Wasn't a family named Hayes heir to the Cannon textile fortunes?

I skipped the morning assignment meeting and drove to Eric's house. I understood exactly why Jack had lied and manipulated the media. But I was still in the dark about Eric's motives.

As I rang his doorbell, I heard raised voices from inside—one high-pitched and shrill, the other low and muffled. Then the voices stopped abruptly, and the front door swung open. A thin brunette wearing yoga pants and a tank top stood in the doorway. "Is . . . is Eric in?" I sounded as if I'd just learned to speak.

"Yes, of course," she said with a British accent. Or was it Australian?

I decided she probably wasn't his sister. Not with that accent. But who was she?

"Who should I tell him is here?" she asked.

Before I could answer, Eric came to the door and ushered me inside.

"Kate." He breathed my name as though he hadn't seen me in years.

"I've seen you on the television news, haven't I?" the brunette asked. "Which station is it?"

"Channel Eleven."

I wondered what she did for a living. The high cheekbones and tall, curveless figure made me think model (or "actor," as models in Los Angeles like to be called). But there was also an iciness to her that made me think ballet dancer.

"You were the one who did the report on Eric's rescue of the boy from the canyon," she continued.

I think I nodded, but I was distracted, trying to figure out her relationship to Eric.

"I'm Patricia Hayes," she said, extending a bony hand.

Hayes. My throat felt raw. Did Eric have a wife? I'd never seen a wedding ring on his finger, never asked.

I didn't like the way she was looking at me, but what was I to do? I shook her hand.

She glanced at her watch. "Good to meet you, Kate, but I have to run," she said in a clipped tone. "Bye, Eric."

She breezed out of the room without even a glance in Eric's direction. His hands twitched nervously. I had the distinct feeling I'd walked in during the middle of a fight. When the door slammed behind her, I knew my hunch was right.

"Was that your wife?" I asked.

He stared at me, clearly stunned by the question. "No," he said finally. "Did you really think that, after everything that's happened between us, I could be married?"

"Nothing would surprise me today," I said quietly.

"That was my brother's wife."

I exhaled in relief, feeling stupid for jumping to conclusions. "I heard arguing."

He raised his eyes toward the ceiling. "Patricia can't forgive me for what happened to Brian. The accident was my fault, Kate."

"Everyone talks about the accident. What happened?"

I barely recognized the voice that came from his throat—strained, as though it took every fiber of his being to talk. "I thought the memory would fade in time. But all these months later, I can see everything, feel everything, as if it happened yesterday."

He sat on the couch, ran his fingers through his hair. He motioned for me to sit next to him, so I did. The silence in the room felt like a heavy curtain that had fallen on us.

"Brian and I took the sailboat—*The Crazy Eight*—out early one morning. It was a bluebird day—no clouds, medium-heavy winds. The Weather Service had predicted a storm later in the afternoon, but we saw no signs of it. But by late afternoon, the sun had disappeared, and a light rain began to fall. The water started getting rough, but we'd been through that channel many times, so we weren't worried.

"Then from out of nowhere the wind kicked up and whipped the sea like a whirling dervish. We turned around, and all we could see was a wall of gray roaring toward us. I'd never seen anything like it. We were pounded by swells as high as twenty feet."

He picked up a small wooden box from the coffee table and twisted it in his hands.

"The boat was crashing from wave to wave, hurling us around the deck. When we looked up, we were headed straight for a reef. We tried to steer away from it, but the wind had become a howling gale, and we couldn't control the boat. We were trying to secure the boom when we slammed into the reef. The boom swung loose, hit Brian in the head, and knocked us both overboard."

He took a deep, shuddering breath and then fell silent, as though weighing whether he should continue.

"The next thing I knew, I was up against the rocky shoreline, and the waves were pummeling me so hard I couldn't breathe. When I close my eyes, I can still remember how loud the wind was, howling like a banshee, and the pounding of the waves crashing against the rocks. The waves were strong—powerful enough to pluck boulders off the shoreline and tumble them in the surf. I knew I wouldn't get out of there alive if I didn't get away from shore. I tried to swim against the current, through it—even around it—but I got nowhere. I kept trying and somehow managed to swim far enough away from shore that I was no longer flung against the rocks with every wave. To this day I don't know how I did it."

His voice became a raspy whisper. "And that's when I made my mistake."

I laid a hand on his thigh for reassurance, but I had the feeling he didn't even know it was there. His eyes had a distant look, as though he were actually seeing the scene he was describing.

"I stayed on the buoy too long."

"The buoy?"

"Brian's lucky buoy was floating in the water. At first I thought I was imagining it, because I couldn't see anything more than a foot or two in front of my face. I grabbed it and hung on through the high waves. I was exhausted but somehow found the strength to hang on to it."

A tear wet the corner of his eye. "But I stayed too long. I wasn't thinking about my brother or how I should have been trying to find him. I was only trying to save myself. That was my mistake—because if I had gone to look for him sooner, he'd still be alive."

His shoulders slumped as though he carried a heavy burden. He looked tired and much older. "When I finally got to him, he was hanging on to a life vest that had fallen from the boat. There was so much blood. Blood everywhere."

He rocked gently back and forth, his hands clenched so tightly that his knuckles were bone white. "But he wasn't dead. Somehow he was alive, even with a six-inch gash that went from his left eyebrow to the back of his head. And he spoke to me. He said . . ."

He closed his eyes tightly and didn't say anything for a long while. When he finally spoke, his voice was shaking. "He said, 'Take care of them for me. Take care of them.' And then he went into cardiac arrest. He was dead. I couldn't save him, Kate. Even though it's what I do for a living. Even though it's what I've trained for my entire life."

I said nothing for a moment, knowing there were no words to say to lessen the pain.

"I should have been able to save him." He turned to look at me. "Remember the accident in the gold mine I told you about?"

I nodded, glancing at the scar that ran the length of his forearm.

"I pulled that man out of the shaft with my arm nearly cut in two. I rescued a boy from thirty-foot waves in Malibu and came out alive. I freed a woman trapped in a burning car suspended from a highway overpass. But I couldn't save my own brother." The muscles in his jaw twitched. "I've put my life in danger in hundreds of rescue operations, and every time I came out alive. Brian never took risks like I did. The only time he did something a little risky, he paid for it with his life. Why was my life spared so many times and Brian's wasn't? It should've been me who drowned that day—not Brian."

I rested my head on his chest, because I didn't know what else to do or say. We were silent then—not an awkward or repressed silence that pressures you to say something, but the kind of silence that comes about naturally when two people are comfortable with each other. A silence of understanding.

"That day I didn't just lose a brother. I lost my sailing partner, my best friend, someone who shared my childhood memories, the one person in the world who'd known me nearly all my life. I lost it all."

I wanted to comfort him and tell him it wasn't his fault. But instinctively I knew no words would make it all better. So I hugged him tightly, like I remember him doing when we went swimming for the first time.

"Let me make you a cup of tea," I said softly.

He nodded but didn't look at me.

I didn't think he was much of a tea drinker, but I wanted to do something to comfort him. As I scrounged around the kitchen cabinets looking for tea bags, my gaze fell upon the buoy in the corner.

I peered at the cracked number eight painted in red on its side and ran my hand along its brittle edge. This was the buoy Eric had clung to during the storm. I wondered why he still had it. Had he kept it here as a constant reminder of his failure to save his brother?

A lump formed in my throat. I can imagine you never really get over losing a brother. And although Eric had done everything possible to save Brian, even that wasn't good enough. In his mind he could have done more.

When I came back with a cup of tea, Eric was silent, staring at his hands.

"Gypsy Cold Care," I said, handing him the mug. "It's the only tea I could find in your cabinets."

"I'm not much of a tea drinker."

"I kind of suspected that. Do you want something else?"

He took a sip of the tea and grimaced. With shaky hands, he set the mug down.

I sat beside him. "I saw the buoy in the kitchen. What happened to *The Crazy Eight*?"

"After the accident, she was completely wrecked. The sails were shredded, and part of the hull was splintered into pieces. I was surprised, though, when the insurance company sent me a check for just over five hundred thousand dollars. I told them they'd made a mistake; the boat had belonged to my brother, not me. But they said that a few weeks before the accident, Brian had transferred ownership to me.

"At first I didn't believe it. Brian had never said anything about giving me the boat. He had his eye on a boat named *Dream*, a fifty-seven-foot Gulfstar yacht, but I never thought he'd let go of his favorite sailboat. Then I remembered him teasing me about a big surprise he was planning for my birthday and realized he had intended to give me *The Crazy Eight*."

"That would be a very generous gift."

"One I didn't deserve," he said quietly. "But Brian was that kind of guy. So when the insurance check came, I tried to give it to Patricia, but she rejected it."

"Why?"

"Brian had plenty of life insurance and lots of real estate, so she didn't need the money. That's what she said back then anyway. She came here today because she'd changed her mind. She wants the money after all. She has two kids to put through college someday. But what I couldn't tell her was that I didn't keep it. It would have been like keeping a dead body in my house, another reminder that my brother wasn't alive to enjoy what he loved most—sailing. I'd failed my brother, and I wasn't about to profit from it. I had to let the money go." He paused. "I considered donating it to a charity. Then I remembered what Brian had said before he died. 'Take care of them.' So I gave it away to the people Brian cared about, the people who truly made a difference in his life."

"His best friend, Larry Durham," I said slowly, as the blur of confusion began to clear. "His babysitter, Cristina Gomez. His reading tutor in college, Lauren Haywood. The doctor who saved his life. And the teacher who helped him to start his own real estate firm."

He nodded silently.

The pieces were falling into place.

"I never expected anyone to find out what I'd done. I never imagined any one of these people would alert the media, and even if they did, I figured it wasn't the kind of story anyone would care about anyway."

I smiled because what he said was true. "And the number eight was stamped on the canvas bags because the boat was named *The Crazy Eight*?"

"Brian had the bags made up after he bought the boat. Turns out they weren't waterproof, so we could never actually use them on the boat," he said. "When someone else began to put money in canvas bags with the number eight on them, I thought it was some kind of cruel mockery of my brother's death."

"Why did you give the money secretly? Why not just tell these people you were giving them money because Brian would've wanted them to have it?"

He shook his head. "I tested the waters and tried to give a few thousand dollars to Larry Durham. But he turned it down. Said it felt too much like taking charity. So I figured the only way to give the money away was to *not* tell any of them where it came from."

A lump formed in my throat as I thought about him placing the money in bags and dropping it anonymously on the five front porches. I thought about the pain he must have experienced when he did it, but also the true generosity that was behind it. "I wish you had told me this earlier."

He looked down at his hands. "I wanted to, but I was afraid of what you would think if you knew the truth. I thought you'd see me for what I was—a failure. Someone who put himself first and let his brother die."

"I see you as someone who did the best you could in terrible circumstances." I pressed my hand to his cheek. "Maybe in time you can forgive yourself. For being human. For being exhausted and afraid when you wanted to be strong and brave."

Eric's eyes locked on mine. "For a long time now I've wanted to tell you the truth about what I'd done. Lying to you like that, day after day, was eating away at me. You have to know that I would never deceive you like that again."

He touched his hand to mine, and his eyes pleaded with me for understanding. And that's when I fell in love with Eric Hayes.

There have been rare moments in my life of such blinding clarity that they are forever engraved in my memory, frozen in time. The day I nearly drowned in Mexico is one of those moments. Falling in love with Eric is another.

It caught me by surprise. Less than twenty-four hours before, I'd walked out on him, convinced he was yet another liar I couldn't trust.

How then could I explain how I felt, wanting him more now than I ever had?

"I never expected my heart to open up to anyone so soon after the accident. But then you came along and changed everything. That's what I meant yesterday when I told you that maybe you were the one rescuing me."

Even though we weren't touching, I felt like we were. He'd shared his deepest grief and opened himself up to me in a way I'd never experienced before. And now I understood. He had been trapped in a drowning machine of his own, and somehow, in a way I couldn't yet comprehend, I had helped rescue him.

He touched his hand to my face, and I felt my anger dissolve. In its place was a new, unfamiliar feeling—the beginnings of forgiveness.

"You can walk out that door again, but that won't change how I feel about you," he said softly. "Nothing will change that."

"I'm not walking out that door." I felt my face grow warm. "Because I think I love you."

I'd always thought that when I finally said those words and meant them, it would have been after long thought and deliberation and with measurable certainty. But they slipped out of my mouth easily and naturally, as though I'd always known it, as if I'd said it many times before.

Over a bottle of wine and some leftover chicken soup, Eric and I talked for hours. He told me more about his life when Brian was alive—weekends and vacations spent sailing with friends, boat trips to Hawaii and Mexico. We talked about my childhood, when I wanted to be just like the girl in *Harriet the Spy*. I told him how I'd put on an oversize yellow raincoat, spied on everyone in the neighborhood, and then returned home to give my father a "report" of everything I'd seen.

"The seeds of my news career were in those reports," I said, "even though I looked silly in that big raincoat."

"I can't imagine that you ever looked silly," he said. His eyes, shining with interest, focused on my face. For once, I didn't fill the silence with words or questions, trying to hold on to the still perfection of the moment.

"What're you thinking?" he asked.

I wasn't sure where to start. I loved that he was Good Sam. He had given anonymously and generously from his heart, without expectation of reward. He was precisely what I thought didn't exist—someone doing good without ulterior motive, not only as Good Sam but every day as a firefighter. At the same time, he wasn't perfect.

I brushed a lazy kiss across his lips. But what started out gentle and tender quickly took on a life of its own. His hands caressed my body. I'd wanted him for so long that I was greedy, wanting to feel all of him, to let the heat that had been building all these weeks between us finally play out.

I'd been in this territory before—groping and rushing, fueled by fire and desire, frantically shedding clothes, racing to get there fast. But we didn't rush. We took our time exploring each other, reining in the need, not knowing how far either of us would take it.

Would he stop as he had the last time we had come this far? Would he just hold me in his arms as we slept the night away under soft covers? As if reading my mind, he whispered, "Do you have any idea what I was thinking the other night?"

I kissed him in the V of his neck. "No, tell me."

"I was thinking how much I wanted to make love with you, but it didn't seem right, knowing I was lying to you. But now that you know everything there is to know about me . . ."

"Not everything," I said quietly. "Not yet, anyway."

Then I answered his unspoken question by tracing the light stubble around his mouth with my fingertips. I covered his mouth with my own, parting his lips with my tongue, our lips and our mouths mingling in a long, lingering kiss.

I wondered what he would be like as a lover. Would he be calculating and careful, like he was on a rescue scene, knowing that everything gained comes from preparation and planning? Or would he be aggressive and wild, taking risks like I'd seen him do as he hung from a wire beneath a helicopter?

He was both—at once tender and rough, in complete control of his body yet abandoned and free with it. And his confidence with his body made me unrestrained with my own, touching him as he touched me, loving him as he loved me.

I felt the power and strength in his arms as he pulled me close, the warmth of him burning into my skin. A wave of uneasiness passed over me as I realized there was no turning back. I was racing full bore down the steepest hill of the roller coaster, and I had to trust him not to break my heart.

Eric lifted his mouth from mine, and we looked at each other for a long moment. As his eyes caught mine in their silent dance, the shaky feeling drifted away.

"I love you, Kate," he said softly.

Men say many things in the throes of passion, but I knew he meant it. I felt it in his every move, saw it in his face.

"I love you, too," I whispered back. I was no longer surprised by how easy it was to say these words—but by how deeply I felt them with each passing moment.

CHAPTER SEVENTEEN

Hours later I awoke tangled in the sheets of Eric's bed. I glanced at him, expecting to find him still sleeping, but instead he was lying on his side, resting his head on his bent arm, looking at me.

"'Morning, beautiful," he said, kissing me.

I glanced at the window. Sunshine burst through the sheer curtains, and I heard the drone of a lawnmower in the distance.

"It's not morning already, is it?" I said, curling my body into his.

"It's already seven."

"How long have you been awake?"

"About an hour," he murmured.

"Why didn't you wake me?"

"I've been watching you sleep, pinching myself every so often to prove I'm not dreaming."

I leaned up and pressed a soft kiss to his lips. Then I hovered next to him for a long moment, breathing in his scent, relaxing into the warmth of his body.

He sat up. "My shift starts at eight, so unfortunately I have to get going."

"You mean you have other people to rescue besides me?"

"Now and then." He ran his strong hand along my arm. "You know, the Chinese believe that when you save a person's life you become their blessed protector, and it's your duty to do that for the rest of your life."

I smiled. "Are you saying that any time I get into a body of water, it's your duty to rescue me?"

"You're stuck with me, yes."

From the way he kissed me then, I knew we both were going to be late for work.

 ⁓

Jack was waiting for me when I arrived at the station that morning. "He's in the conference room," the receptionist said. "Been here for an hour."

I frowned. There'd be no time to even grab a cup of coffee.

"Would you let David know I need to see him?" I said, heading upstairs to the conference room.

Jack had shuttered all the blinds in the glass-enclosed conference room and turned out all the overhead lights, so only a small halogen lamp on the credenza lit up the room. I paused a moment to allow my eyes to adjust to the dark.

"Where have you been?" he said hoarsely. "I've left messages for you everywhere. I even waited in front of your house late last night, but you never came home."

I'd never seen him like this before. An air of desperation clung to him, his shirtsleeves rolled to his elbows, light wrinkles in his Savile Row trousers.

"Your receptionist said you're always on time. Eight o'clock sharp every day. It's nearly nine. Where have you been?"

A sharp chill seeped into my bones. "Why do you want to know?"

His eyes flashed angrily. "We left things on a sour note the other night. I want to talk about it."

I sat in the chair beside him. "There's nothing to talk about."

"Then you've decided *not* to tell the Good Sam story?"

"No, I'm still going through with it."

"Don't," he said. It was the first time I actually felt frightened of him. "You'll kill my chance to win this seat in Congress, and you'll ruin my reputation—not to mention your own." He ran his fingers through his already tousled hair. "What does the 'real' Good Sam think about your telling the story?"

"I didn't ask."

"I'm sure he won't like it, either. Did he tell you why he gave all that money away?"

"Yes."

"Why did he do it?"

"I can't say."

"It won't be private once you tell your story. You'll expose him, too. Don't you see, Kate? Everyone loses if you tell the truth. You will. I will. He will."

Jack was right. Everyone would lose if I told the truth, especially me. But how could I call myself a reporter if I concealed the truth?

"Don't do it." Jack pleaded in a rough whisper. "Don't do this to us."

"There is no *us*, Jack."

He closed his eyes as if to shut out my words. His shoulders slumped and his jaw slackened. For the first time, I saw a defeated Jack Hansen. As much as I'd once fantasized about seeing him like this after he'd hurt me and lied to me, looking at him now only made me sad.

We sat in icy silence. The sound of the door opening caught our attention. A sliver of light from the hallway pierced the heavy gloom in the room. David poked his head in the doorway. "Kate, were you looking for me?"

"Yes," I answered and then turned to Jack. "I have to go, Jack."

He nodded and stared straight ahead.

As I walked out of the room, I felt his eyes upon me, begging me to do the right thing.

∽

I told David everything. As I spelled out the details of the true Good Sam story, he rubbed one ear and then the other, something I'd never seen him do before.

When I finished, his words cut into me like a knife. "We're screwed—you, me, anyone who worked on the damn story. When Bonnie hears about this, she'll have us out of here so fast our heads will spin."

"Maybe there's a way—"

"No." The volume of his voice went up a notch. "This is the kind of mistake that brings news organizations down, that ruins reputations and kills careers. This isn't going to fade away."

"What if we—"

"Damn it." He slammed his fist on his desk. "How the hell did you let Jack Hansen put this over on us?"

"Maybe we wanted to believe too much—not just us, but the viewers, too," I said quietly. "Every newscast we report on murders, assaults, shootings, robberies—the terrible things people do to each other. Maybe we were caught off guard when someone appeared to be doing something truly good for other people. When a dynamic man comes forward and admits he did it, we want to believe him, because believing convinces us that maybe there is good out there after all."

David stared at me and stopped rubbing his ears.

"Don't tell Bonnie yet," I continued in a calm voice, even though my heart was slamming against my ribs. "Let me put together my story. Then we'll let her decide."

I felt light-headed as I walked back to my desk. So much was riding on what I did in the next hours, and I felt pretty sure I'd pass out before I got to do any of it.

Shondra stopped me in the hallway. "You've got another visitor. Eric Hayes. I sent him to your desk."

I smiled this time and rushed into the newsroom.

"Can't stay long," he whispered. "The truck is parked out front, and my team is waiting for me. But we just finished training on the LA River, and I was thinking about you."

"Thinking about what you're going to do the next time I fall into the river?"

"Missing you."

His smile made my heart race. Then more sobering thoughts came to mind.

"There's something I have to do today, Eric. Something you won't like. I have to tell the real story about Good Sam. Viewers have to know the truth . . . but it means telling your story."

The smile faded from his face. "I don't want anyone to know who I am or why I did it."

"Will you let me interview you?"

He looked at me with an expression of confusion and uncertainty. I knew what he was going to say, but it didn't make it easier when the words came out of his mouth.

"No," he said quietly. "I'd do just about anything for you, Kate. Anything. But not that."

I was silent then, wishing I could run away from the newsroom and from this story and pretend I'd never heard of Good Sam. It was bad enough that my own career would go down in flames when I told the truth, but hurting Eric in the process was too high a price to pay.

Was the truth really so important?

I sat at my computer in the newsroom for several hours, trying to figure out what to say in the report I had promised David. Most of that time, I'd stared at the blank computer screen, the cursor blinking at me as if in warning. Would this be the last report I'd file for Channel Eleven—or for any television station? Would viewers think we had deceived them by wrongly putting forth Jack Hansen as Good Sam?

I finished my third cup of my coffee and crumpled the cup in my hands. The screen—my script—was blank. How could I tell the story without revealing Eric was Good Sam?

"Something's definitely going on around here," Alex said, startling me. He placed another cup of coffee on my desk and slid into the chair next to me. "Because David's been behind closed doors with Bonnie all morning. And you haven't said a word to anyone in two hours. During my entire internship, I don't think I've seen you even sit down for more than fifteen minutes."

I cracked my first smile of the day. "You've got great observation skills, Alex. You're going to make a great reporter."

He smiled. "It's bad news, isn't it?"

"Definitely bad news." I repeated, tapping my pen on my desk. But was it? What viewers loved about the Good Sam story was that an anonymous person was doing something generous and good. *That hadn't changed.*

I leapt out of my chair and ran down the hallway to see if dispatch would assign Josh to be my cameraman. Luckily, he had just finished covering an ammonia spill at a cheese factory and was ready to go. I explained what had happened as we headed to Cristina Gomez's house. Instead of shock or dismay or even anger, Josh broke into a huge smile.

"Remember the day when we first reported on Good Sam? We thought he was just giving randomly. But knowing that it wasn't random—that the real Good Sam had chosen those people for a specific reason—is way more meaningful."

I didn't need a script or notes as I stood in front of Cristina Gomez's house with its fresh coat of paint and newly repaired front porch and recorded the report.

"In the early-morning hours of a cold January day three weeks ago, a man placed a canvas bag containing one hundred thousand dollars in cash on this porch. He gave the money anonymously, leaving no clues regarding his identity. He repeated this gesture four more times, giving away more than five hundred thousand dollars in a few days' time.

"We called this man 'Good Sam.' Intrigued by this selfless gesture, we and other media outlets around the country tried to find out who he was.

"When Jack Hansen came forward and admitted he was Good Sam, he gave me proof, but I didn't examine it in minute detail. Accustomed to covering the police blotter of murders and accidents and shootings, I was caught off guard when dealing with someone who was doing so much good.

"But Jack Hansen isn't Good Sam. Yes, he was generous—giving away a total of five hundred thousand dollars to five residents *after* the attention to Good Sam reached a fever pitch. He did this in order to launch a career in politics.

"Then who is the real Good Sam?

"Unlike Hansen, he isn't a millionaire or a political candidate. He didn't do it for the visibility, the attention, or the exposure. He did it as a silent tribute to the brother he lost in a tragic accident last year—to honor his brother's dying wish to take care of the people he loved. He gave the money to the man who had been his brother's best friend since fourth grade, to the tutor who had helped his brother with a reading problem in college, to the teacher who had encouraged his brother to start his own business, to the babysitter who had taken care of his brother's sick child while he worked, and to the surgeon who had once saved his brother's life. These were the people who made his brother's life richer, stronger, better. And he could think of no better way to honor his brother than to give to those who had made a difference in his brother's life.

"Who is the real Good Sam who showed us the meaning of true generosity? If we tell you who he is, we will have defeated his efforts to give anonymously. So for now we'll let the identity of the anonymous Good Sam remain just that—anonymous."

CHAPTER EIGHTEEN

On a moonlit night Eric and I glided over the open sea. The only sound was the creaking of the tall mast, the hush of the sails above our heads, and the burbling of the water against the hull. Stirred by our passage, small jellyfish and sea creatures twinkled and glowed in the dark waters below, creating the illusion that we were suspended in space.

I never expected to feel at home here with just a few inches of fiberglass between the deep blue sea and me. But we'd defeated the water once, Eric and I, and after a few more swimming lessons and sailing trips, I'd begun to make an uneasy peace with the water. I'd grown accustomed to the sound of it lapping at the hull, the rhythmic sway of the boat on the open sea, the foamy wake behind us, and the salty taste of it on my lips. And I'd begun to appreciate the boat as a temporary island, a place where spirits are buoyed by the open air, the endless sky, and the possibilities that lie in the inky darkness ahead.

Eric came alive here, his body tuned to every nuance of the boat he'd made his own a few months ago. He'd named her *Andromeda* and seemed to anticipate her every need, letting her rest and almost hover on the water when the air died down and pushing her to the limits when the winds were right. I admired his ability to respond to the unseen—the winds, the air pressure, the lay of the water—whether we sailed through mist and spray and smudgy skies or puffy clouds and blue waters.

Six weeks had passed since Good Sam had captured the nation's attention. Once the public knew the truth about what Jack did, he quickly withdrew his bid for Congress. The five people who had received money from Eric as a tribute to his brother gathered with him and Brian's wife one night to remember the ways in which Brian had touched their lives. The evening had brought healing for Eric, but his grief and his guilt were far from over. We had talked for many hours about what had happened on the boat that fateful day in June, and I suspected that it would be a part of our lives for a long time to come.

As for me, I wasn't fired from Channel Eleven. I'd played my report for Bonnie and David, and they were surprisingly supportive, scheduling it at the top of the six o'clock cast. David even went out on a limb to say, "Well done, Kate." But the bigger battle lay ahead with the viewers. I had expected them to be outraged about being duped by Jack Hansen and angry with me for putting him forward as the real thing. Some were. But many couldn't get enough of the story about the real Good Sam and his reasons for giving away the money. The story touched them in a way they hadn't expected, reminded them that relationships and caring for others were more important than ambition and fame.

The social media channels lit up with theories about who Good Sam was. Some posited conspiracy theories, while others claimed various celebrities were behind the amazing story. A few people managed to guess correctly, but the obsession with Good Sam's identity faded as people started focusing more on the copycat Good Sams popping up around the country.

A Good Sam had gone to work in Muncie, Indiana, leaving a thousand dollars in the mailboxes of five public school teachers. Another had surfaced in Stillwater, Minnesota, giving five thousand dollars to Clarence Whistler, who had mowed the lawn and wound the historic clock in the bell tower once a week for twenty-three years as a janitor at the county courthouse. Every day new stories rolled in. At one point, Alex had calculated that copycat Good Sams around the country had given away more than three million dollars in increments as small as one hundred dollars.

As I leaned against the railing at the bow of the boat, breathed in the cool, salty air, and watched the moon dance along the whitecaps, I wasn't thinking about Jack Hansen, Good Sam, or reporting the news. I was thinking how lucky I was to have found the man steering the boat tonight.

Over the years, I'd convinced myself that good rarely exists in this world, and if it does, it comes with ulterior motives and hidden agendas. But the truth is that good is everywhere. It's harder to see, but often it's right in front of you.

Or in this case, behind me. Eric wrapped his strong arms around my waist. He pointed at a group of stars above us. "Can you see Perseus holding the head of Medusa?"

I squinted, using every ounce of imagination to see the Gorgon's snake-filled head in the sprinkle of stars. "Maybe."

"And do you see Andromeda to Perseus's right?"

I saw her, still and bright in the night sky. "Yes."

"Maybe you're ready to start learning how to navigate the boat by the stars," he said, squeezing me gently.

"Give me time," I said, smiling. "I've got a taskmaster for a swimming instructor who's pushing me to learn the butterfly and the overarm sidestroke. After I've mastered all that, perhaps I'll be ready learn to navigate a boat by the stars."

Eric was silent as he nuzzled my hair. "We're like them, you know."

"Like who?"

"Like Perseus and Andromeda. You were Andromeda being swallowed up by the sea, and I was Perseus, flying down and slaying the sea monster to rescue you."

I turned to look at him. "Except I wasn't chained to a rock."

He smiled and kissed me. "Always a stickler for the truth, aren't you?"

I kissed him back. "What happened to Perseus and Andromeda after he rescued her?"

"Andromeda's parents promised Perseus a kingdom as a dowry for marrying her."

"Hmm. I don't have a dowry. Or a kingdom. So I guess our story isn't the same after all."

"I'd take you without either," he said quietly. My eyes met his in the soft light coming from the ship's cabin. "If you'd have me."

"Are you asking—"

He grinned. "Yes, for once I'm the one asking the questions."

I kissed him then—a kiss that left me breathless in its depth and its meaning.

FROM THE AUTHOR

I wrote *Good Sam* because I wanted to explore a mystery where characters search for someone doing anonymous good instead of the usual killers and kidnappers. I never imagined that the novel I wrote in the late hours of the night after my kids were asleep would go on to win four book awards, become a bestseller, and be made into a film for the Hallmark Channel.

Readers like you made that happen. Readers who believe in the importance of seeking out and illuminating good in the world—who write reviews and encourage friends and family to read *Good Sam*. For that, I'm forever grateful.

But Kate and Eric's journey doesn't end with *Good Sam*. Pick up the award-winning follow-up, *Perfectly Good Crime*, which has been featured in *Parade*, *Sunset*, BuzzFeed, *Working Mother*, and many other top publications.

When the estates of the one hundred wealthiest Americans are targeted in a series of sophisticated, high-tech heists, Los Angeles TV news reporter Kate Bradley must venture inside the world of the superrich to investigate the biggest story of the year.

As the heists escalate, Kate's search is thwarted when the Los Angeles police detective she's been working with mysteriously disappears, her senator father demands that she stop reporting on the heists, and the billionaire victims refuse to talk to the media. Kate uncovers clues that those behind the robberies have shocking, yet uplifting, motives—it just may be a perfectly good crime that brings about powerful change.

Further complicating her life is a dream job awaiting her in New York, a choice that could shatter her deepening relationship with fire captain Eric Hayes. Kate must trust her instincts—and her heart—in a high-stakes search that will test everything she believes and force her to decide where she belongs.

Thank you for spending your time with *Good Sam*. I hope you'll read *Perfectly Good Crime*!

> Yours,
>
> Dete

Stay in touch:

Website: DeteMeserve.com

E-mail: DeteMeserve@gmail.com

For stories about real-life Good Sams, follow me on Facebook: Facebook.com/GoodSamBook

Twitter: @DeteMeserve

ACKNOWLEDGMENTS

Several years ago, my friend and KNBC News reporter, Laurel Erickson, invited me to spend a day with her "riding along," as she covered the news for NBC4 in Los Angeles. What started as a routine day covering a story about water use on a golf course quickly became a breaking-news story when an elderly man plowed his car through a busy farmer's market in Santa Monica, killing ten and injuring sixty-three others. Laurel quickly went into action, covering the chaotic scene and putting me to work to find people who would talk with her about what they'd seen. Watching Laurel that day, calm and assured as she covered this tragic event, was a great inspiration for the character of Kate Bradley.

Good Sam was also inspired by the real-life heroism of Larry Collins, battalion chief and a leader of the Los Angeles County Fire Department's Urban Search and Rescue Task Force. Larry received the distinguished Medal of Valor from the Los Angeles County Fire Department for the rescue of a building inspector trapped in a sixty-foot-deep vertical shaft. One of the rescue scenes in the story was based on this event; others were drawn from countless dramatic rescues Larry performed. Larry's humble inability to see the extraordinary courage of his rescue efforts inspired the character of Eric Hayes.

I'm also thankful to friends who shared their insight and thoughtful feedback on early drafts of the novel: Debra Gaynor, Kes Trester, Barbara Schroeder, Joan Singleton, Larry Collins, Phyllis Kincaid, Hannah

Stein Whitney, Zehavah Oates, Devorah and Robert Heyman, Lisa Wainland, and Lori Costew. Many thanks to my advisers and experts: Jesseca Salky at Lyons & Salky Law, LLP, Elizabeth Hopkins and Steve Monas at Business Affairs, Inc., and Daniel Peterson at Artesian Design. Special thanks to my editors Angela Brown and Miriam Juskowicz and the entire Lake Union Publishing Team.

ABOUT THE AUTHOR

 Like her heroine Kate Bradley, award-winning author Dete Meserve keeps looking for people who are doing extraordinary good for others, sometimes at great personal sacrifice. Instead of tracking a killer or kidnapper, Dete's mysteries seek to uncover the helpers, the rescuers, and the people who inspire us with selfless acts of kindness. *Good Sam* is the first in her Kate Bradley Mysteries series, followed by *A Perfectly Good Crime.*

When she's not writing, Dete is a film and television producer and a partner in Wind Dancer Films. She lives in Los Angeles with her husband and three children—and a very good cat that rules them all. For more on the author and her work, visit www.detemeserve.com or connect with her on Twitter @DeteMeserve and on Facebook at Facebook.com/GoodSamBook.